David G. Hernández Gómez
Written as D.G.H.G.
All rights reserved © 1995-2023

TABLE OF CONTENTS

DEDICATION

To no one.

ACKNOWLEDGEMENTS

The following is a list of people who either supported me throughout this book's creative process or, in one way or the other, indirectly inspired its creation. The names are in no specific order or belong to a particular group.

O. I. Gómez (MB), R. Gómez, S.A. Gómez, G. Hernández, Melisa R., L.E. Domenech, I.O. Pellot, Natasha Nicole R., Alice F., Angel F., Joana L., Marilyn S., A. Acosta, Dancore Jiménez, Tico J., Melanie C., Dianelis S., Duaine, Suleimy L., C.R. Cardona, Mariel R., Yashira Marie, N. Binet., G. Millayes, J. Rodríguez, B.J. Rodríguez, J. Valentín, Fabi M.T., L. Omar S., D. Herencia, Nilsy F., C.M. Boscio, Aimée B., G. Cortez, Pete Gónzalez, A. Cortez, Mark N., Cesar S., C. Badillo, D. Monroig, M. Cruz, Darwin C., Elvin A., Eric R., Gabriela R., Glouribel R., Gustavo H., Hans G., Gigi Pérez, Hector, Higinio M., I. Rojas. Marisol A., M. Montalvo, Javariz, J. Domenech, J. Muñíz, J. Goyco, J. Méndez, J.I. Crespo, Lily G., M. Lasaney, M. Martínez, J. Pares. M. Rondon, O. Montelera, Nashaly R., Lilo R, T.Guzmán, Victor R., Zahilia M., Gregorio L., Osorio, Ana Chan, Edia L. S., Eric G., Gerald F., M.D.M. González, Maritza G., Mike M., Nikko B., Sergio A., Tatiana Anelisse, Tairaliz M., Xiomara L, A. R. Redington.

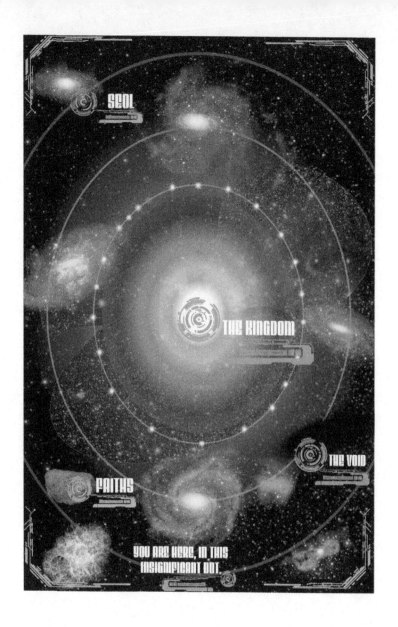

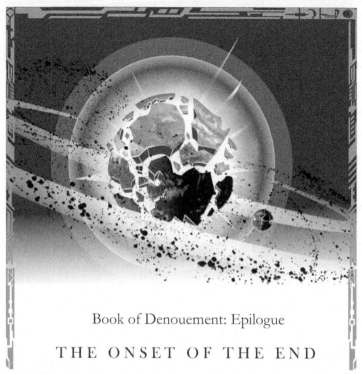

Book of Denouement: Epilogue

THE ONSET OF THE END

"I SEE IT IN THE DISTANCE—rippling curtains made of shooting rays that light up the cosmos with mixing colors and an unnerving glow. It's an unsettling visual spectacle that forewarns spectators that the ***Known Universe*** is in extremis. All existing interstellar matter is at the point of death. As the Universe draws its final breath, death rides onward, unstoppable and unseen. The feeling is palpable. The shivering air carries a ghastly shriek and leaves behind a nauseating reek of decay. The eroding wave forged of pure wroth and malice transverses the Universe

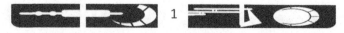

forthwith, leaving nothing but necrotic particles of stardust in its wake. Eons turn to dust that dissipates like dandelions in the air. Memories and remnants of history are forever gone. That which once was would never be again. Erstwhile, there has always been a resurgence, another chance to start anew. After the onslaught of this particular Armageddon, there will NOT be another beginning. On this day, there will be no resurrection, transcendence of spirits, or second coming.

The cancerous darkness has metastasized across the cosmos, endlessly consuming every spec of life. The blitzkrieg assault is felt by every living organism, as it devours both the insentient—those incapable of having a basic understanding beyond their biological roles—and all conscious creatures alike. For the affrighted beings who have triumphed over the inferior ones by ascending a step above them on the evolutionary ladder, this moment is when the erratic notion of control and all fictional concepts of self-awareness develop to justify an existence without purpose come undone. Both the irreverent, the blasphemous, the profane, and their opposite, the chosen, those so-called righteous, the humble, the enduring ones who, after a lifetime of long-suffering are still willing to

follow a gospel teaching to archive a justified reward, equally fall to the crumbling ground beneath them. They claw deep into the soil, clinging desperately to life on the brink of extinction.

The radiated windstorm distorts their faces beyond recognition, peeling flesh from bone and eroding bone to dust. Millions of lifeforms across the galaxy are atomized and cast off like ashes in the wind.

The end is near. As I float above the ruins of humankind's most outstanding architectural achievement, I can feel it all around me. I look to my left and see that even the hulking immortal beside me knows it. Keeled down, benumbed by pain, this once phenomenal warrior cradles the empty arm socket where his muscular right arm used to be. Even though he has won the day, now he is defeated by circumstances beyond his control. With watery eyes, he stares deeply into infinity, awaiting the inevitable. For us, the last two living souls that abide in this mass grave, all that is left to do is wait for the inevitable end.

"I am *Malefactor*, the patron saint of ungodly deeds. Finally, my time has come." — *S. Malefactor*

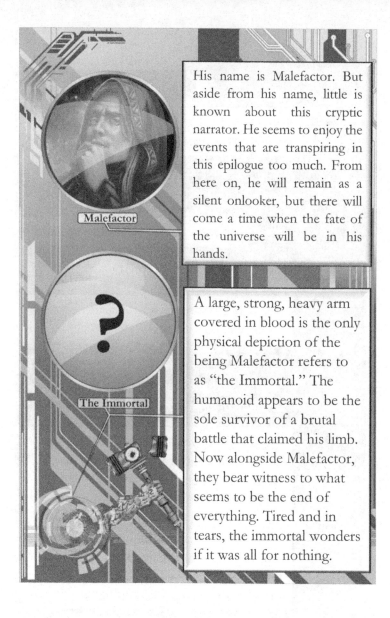

Malefactor

His name is Malefactor. But aside from his name, little is known about this cryptic narrator. He seems to enjoy the events that are transpiring in this epilogue too much. From here on, he will remain as a silent onlooker, but there will come a time when the fate of the universe will be in his hands.

The Immortal

A large, strong, heavy arm covered in blood is the only physical depiction of the being Malefactor refers to as "the Immortal." The humanoid appears to be the sole survivor of a brutal battle that claimed his limb. Now alongside Malefactor, they bear witness to what seems to be the end of everything. Tired and in tears, the immortal wonders if it was all for nothing.

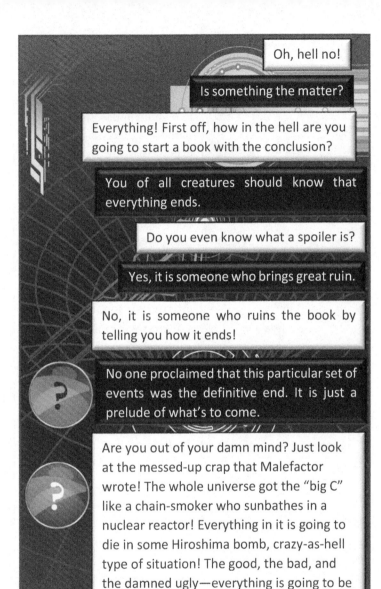

Oh, hell no!

Is something the matter?

Everything! First off, how in the hell are you going to start a book with the conclusion?

You of all creatures should know that everything ends.

Do you even know what a spoiler is?

Yes, it is someone who brings great ruin.

No, it is someone who ruins the book by telling you how it ends!

No one proclaimed that this particular set of events was the definitive end. It is just a prelude of what's to come.

Are you out of your damn mind? Just look at the messed-up crap that Malefactor wrote! The whole universe got the "big C" like a chain-smoker who sunbathes in a nuclear reactor! Everything in it is going to die in some Hiroshima bomb, crazy-as-hell type of situation! The good, the bad, and the damned ugly—everything is going to be turned into one massive skid-mark!

As I said, the end is inevitable.

Yeah, but you should save some of that insane stuff for the third book or the final season.

I fail to see how waiting before or after the harvest affects the results.

It's like talking to a damn turkey! Look, you are missing the point. You cannot start a story by telling the reader how it ends. The narrator of this chapter is crazy as hell, floating about celebrating the end of life, while we have a huge, muscular guy with one arm crying about who knows what. Is that supposed to be the hero?

Both are protagonists in an unlikely story. One of these two characters will shape the future you see before you. The other will be the unsuspected instrument to bring it about. Two sides of a coin, chaos and order, and yes, villain and hero, respectively.

So, our limbless hero won the battle, but now the universe is taking it up the chocolate highway, so he is good as dead? I hope there's some character development going forward, or I'm telling you, I'm going to blow a damn gasket!

TIME

FOR MOST, time is an irreversible stream of light—cogs on a clock that turns on a guaranteed path that never strays. Seconds, minutes, and hours are a mortal's measurement for moments that follow another, like knots on a string, and once a moment dissipates, it is gone forever.

For a thing like me, a disembodied voice in the shadows, time is but pages on a book. The past, present, and future are sheets of paper I can randomly turn to at any given point.

Now imagine the listlessness that arises from reading one single book throughout infinity. I have memorized every birth, death, rise, and fall of all living things subsisting in this plane of existence and beyond. Granted that there are creatures given the boon of choice, 'free will' some call it. Although in the grand scheme of life, those choices may cause a diverse set of circumstances within the same environment, it is all for nothing. Self-determination is a myth. Within this cursed canonical Universe, all possibilities and timelines converge into one outcome.

This moment, however, is one of great importance. Of all points in time, a pivotal event such as this merits rereading. After all, how often does one witness a deity questioning its own beliefs?

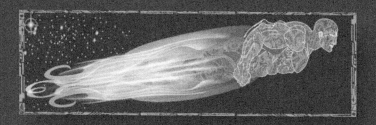

A single Traveler breezes through the vastness of space as he is accustomed to, defiantly and unchecked. His godlike hubris has led him to believe he is entitled to know the answers he seeks. Suddenly, his quest for knowledge is abruptly halted by my gravelly voice that echoes all around him.

"Traveler, your life compass is broken beyond repair."

The Traveler halts in midflight, looking for the source of the horrifying voice that haunts him.

"Where is your north, Traveler? Is it missing, or has it led you astray?"

The Traveler holds his head as if it were to burst, contemplating that he has gone insane.

In such a short time, life-altering, concurrent events have transpired in his life. He belongs to a species that has been the object of worship by some for having power over controlling gods' and mortals' fortunes. The overseer of order now finds himself in an existential crisis.

"I guarantee you, Traveler, you are not out of the deep end quite yet. However, the pursuit of truth has led you across the cosmos, unaware that the truth you seek is much like this place. A hole in the Universe. A bottomless void deprived of stars and filled with darkness."

"Who dares?" the Traveler utters boldly while his inner core shivers like the last autumn leaf trembles before the howling, cold winds of winter.

"Dare? You felt my presence before I uttered a single word, yet you addressed me like a pebble on your pathway, a minor nuisance blocking your trail. Traveler, I am the inevitable end."

For the first time in his long life, the Traveler, a creature of vast power who has paved the destiny of millions, succumbs to emotions known only by his underlings. His essence grew perverted by rage, and his courage was corrupted by fear.

"From above and below, I am the foremost authority! You! You who play in the shadows know this. Generations will come and go! However, only three things shall remain—the Universe, order, and I!" the Traveler answers with an authoritarian mandate, yet he seems to choke on his words as they break upon his quivering lips.

"Your authority is that of a mud-monkey!"

This statement will surely rile him up, for there is no creature more detestable to an ethereal than a human.

"I know not who or what you are, but by the authority bequeathed to me, I demand that you reveal yourself!" proclaims the irate Traveler.

A burst of light emanates from the Traveler's hands to form a complex sigil. The ancient circles and symbols composed of pretty lights accomplish nothing.

The Traveler is perplexed as he hovers amidst space, moving and tilting his head at an unnatural speed, looking to no avail for the source of the spectral voice that haunts him.

"You demand? You have a skewed perception of your importance!" The Traveler widens his eyes and is taken aback by my words. "To me, a creature like you is the equivalent of a convalescent bug on the floor. Nevertheless, even the most ordinary beings have a role to play."

The Traveler braces himself for another attack. His inner core radiates a bountiful amount of energy while his fists and eyes glow like the blinding light of dawn, and he issues a stern warning to the voice that haunts him.

"I am no one to trifle with, Ghost! Who are you?"

Even though he will dislike my retort, the light spectacle is to attitudinize, a show of force to establish dominance—like when a simple-minded primate beats his chest. I answer the Traveler as best as I can.

"Now that is a very long story, Traveler."

The Traveler and primates share common distinguishing characteristics: curiosity and outbursts of violence. Unbeknownst to him, his desire to acquire answers to the questions that plague his existence will eventually outweigh his temper.

"Enlighten me, then," says the Traveler sarcastically.

For me, the time has come for a simple voice in the dark to shatter the Traveler's frail reality.

"Very well then, listen closely, for I have much to say."

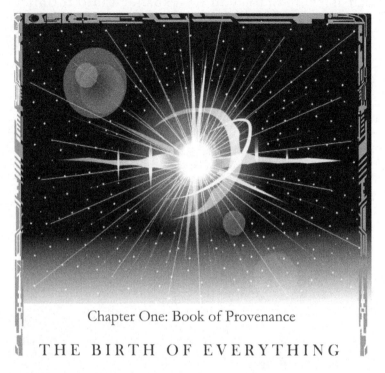

Chapter One: Book of Provenance

THE BIRTH OF EVERYTHING

HOW EVERYTHING CAME TO BE is shrouded in mystery, for those who witnessed the beginning are long gone, and the prophets who professed the event twist the facts to assert control of the masses. I remember it as it was because even though I once shunned it, the source has always been a part of me.

A flash of light flickering in the distance was the first sight of his coming. Smaller than a quark, this mass of blinding light began eddying and

pulsing, and within less than a second, everything that is, was, and would be, expanded into infinity.

The Known Universe was forged out of a cosmic singularity, an eruption of cosmic energy that originated in a single point and expanded every way, haphazardly and perpetually. The unknown and all-powerful being, forged from nothingness and wherefrom everything else came to be, would be forever known as the causeless source, for this Universe is the origin of all things and, therefore, is before all else. If it is to have no purpose outside of itself, then it is eternal in its existence. Not only is there no time when the Universe was not, but its very existence transcends time, for space-time originated from the same singularity, and the Universe exists outside the dimension of time.

"I don't need a history lesson, Ghost! The origin of the *Supreme Being* is universally known! I should know. By his hand, I came to be, and his will is my own."

"Remarkable. Ignorance and arrogance truly go hand in hand. Shush now, Traveler! This is not the creator of whom you speak."

The Universe is a living entity. Its omnipresence is felt by every living creature that inhabits it, from microorganisms to the simplest single-cell organisms chosen to evolve into something more. In one way or the other, they all sense its existence.

Though some creatures, like the *"Pan'soph'ics,"* brilliant cosmographers who archived the highest accumulation of knowledge in the known galaxy, have transcended beyond the need for a spiritual  connection. In their hubris, they've disregarded this universal force as just a place. Blinded by their limited senses, they've reduced life into simple numerical equations.

Unbeknownst to them, there are miraculous creatures of vast power, like the *Caelestis*.

"You know of them, Ghost? The *Caelestis*. Where are they?" the Traveler asks me in a necessitous manner.

"You are a rash creature, Traveler, seldom seen in those granted immortality. The Caelestis are remarkable creatures and quite resourceful too. You need not worry about finding them. In due time they will find you."

The Traveler's chest contracts in an effortful manner. His bloodcurdling scream is muffled only by sheer arrogance.

Indoctrinated as the rightful protectors of the Universe are the Caelestis. These caretakers of the cosmos remain inert and away from the curious eyes of all living things until a time comes when they will wake to decimate any threats.

"You're mistaken, Ghost! We are the truthful guardians of the Universe! This task was appointed to us by the divine command of the *Supreme Being*," states the heated Traveler.

"Divine command is just a rephrase for sanctified atrocious acts. You are but nitwitted creatures that play with forces beyond your scope of comprehension. You and your kin are not saviors, Traveler. You are instruments of destruction."

"You cannot pass judgment upon me, Ghost, for I am part of the Law-Lords, those who magistrate the living!"

"And yet you, Traveler, a creature that does not belong, can pass judgment over those who do."

"Your tendency to speak in riddles is infuriating, Ghost."

"I am talking about anima, Traveler. Something you and your kin undoubtedly lack. A thing like you, overseeing those who can connect to the Universe, is much like an infant masterminding an adult's life."

The Traveler throws another tantrum, and more pretty lights come with it. I must make haste, for they will be here soon.

"I would like to continue if you are finished."

The Traveler still fails to comprehend that there are indeed powers that dwarf his own. Control and manipulation are quintessential parts of him. Right now, he lacks authority. So, he lashes out as a toddler would when someone takes away his toy.

"Your kin had manipulated the destiny of others for eons Traveler, and yet you know very little of these creatures. Allow me to explain."

The rest of the Universe's inhabitants, those born of anima, the divine connection that unites the living to the Life Bringer, can embrace their spirituality. Those who elect to join with the Universe can acquire a taste of cosmic mindfulness by reaching out with little effort. Those who do so with sincerity can archive enlightenment and enter a state of deep tranquility and kindness. Creatures who are inherently meek are often infused by goodness and faithfulness.

However, life cannot abide without balance, for causality deeply entwines with everything that is and forever will be. Thus, a counterpart of the Universe also came into existence.

Deep within space, in the utmost darkest corner of the cosmos, a wicked creature came forth. The foul and gangrenous presence, formed of pure malevolence, made its existence known throughout the galaxy. Just like the Universe erupted violently into being, so did it.

"Utter nonsense!" the Traveler yells.

Overwhelmed by my narrative, he aimlessly shoots beams of beautiful lights at the pitch-black void that surrounds him—blasting away erratically at a hole in space. Suddenly he halts his assault and goes numb. He stares directly at the Void, and his gaze falls upon the darkness. Still agitated, he remembers that before I uttered a single word to him, the Traveler already knew that something was wrong with what he was led to believe. His doctrine is flawed.

"Are you quite finished with your tantrum?" I ask the Traveler as he remains unaware of my voice's origin. "I am a patient creature. I am eternal. I can wait, until the end of time, until the last star of the cosmos bursts, and you dissipate with it."

The Traveler elevates his gaze in anger. Instinctively, he knows something is wrong with the tale he has always known. However, the notion of entertaining an alternate view of how everything came to be is still implausible to him—a nuance shared by hidebound creatures. Hitherto, his life makes no sense, and a morbid curiosity compels him to listen.

"You have a vivid imagination, Ghost. You're nothing but a coward that holes up in the shadows and spits utter profanities! Finish your tale and show yourself so I can teach you some manners!"

He is still very much afraid. Unable to hide his fear any longer, he has chosen anger as his ally, a temporary armor to deflect the nothingness of loss. The Traveler's faith crumbles before him.

"Allow me to continue my narrative, as this part is pivotal."

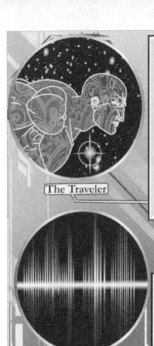

The Traveler

This creature of unknown origin claims to be a Law-Lord and guardian of the universe. He oversees the life of many, including gods and humanoids. He currently navigates the cosmos, seeking answers that can renew his faith.

A Voice In The Shadows

Our narrator is a disembodied voice that can see the past, present, and future. She claims to know the origin of The Known Universe. A truth that clashes with the Traveler's beliefs, an opportunity she gladly uses to humiliate him.

The Pan'soph'ics

They are creatures of utmost brilliance. In the grand scheme of the Universe, these beings will have a small but valuable role to play in the long run.

What a douche!

What seems to be troubling you now, Marie Morana Mallory?

Yeah, that's not my name.

Was that not your given name on your last incarnation?

Yup, but I go by "Ru-Vi-Flo."

An interesting moniker. An amalgamation of the three names of the witches in Macbeth. Very proper, considering that you burned during the time of the witch-hunts.

Mac who?

sighs

That whole thing was a misunderstanding. First off, Monsieur Muet had it coming! Every day that old rat passed the monastery, agitating and cussing at the poor pigs!

Until the day you readied the pigs and unleashed them at him.

Yup. There was a trial and everything.

I saw. The humans put you and the pigs on trial for murder. Seeing a pig testifying is quite something.

Yeah. Snowflake had my back, but Napoleon was a snitch! So many oinks, so many lies. In the end, it was all about money. The loss of all those pigs was something Friar Humbert couldn't afford, so he wrote to the Duke, pleading to pardon the pigs. Long story short, Snowflake and I got turned to bacon. But I stand before you as a pig advocate.

Your headstone reads: "Witch and a cohort of the devil."

Dammit!

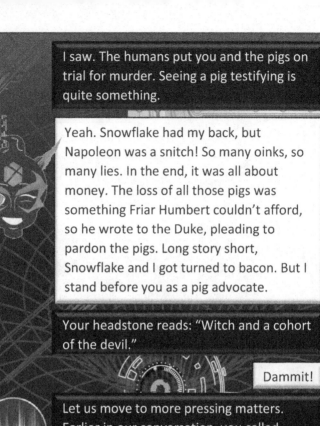

Let us move to more pressing matters. Earlier in our conversation, you called someone a "douche." I take it that you are referring to a contemptible person in particular.

Yeah, That bold-headed Traveler. What an annoying, snobby know-it-all.

Hardheadedness is indeed a trait found in the ways of fundamentalists. Some things are deemed unquestionable by authoritarian decree, and some creatures are more than willing to believe them even in the absence of reasonable knowledge. Every creature is responsible for unlearning the habits that dwarf their mental growth. The Traveler is not yet ready to let go of these beliefs.

What a moron!

I wouldn't be so judgmental.

Why?

He might have a stern, warped view of universal law, but you were human. Humans are a worsening epidemic with no redeemable qualities. As of now, there isn't a remote place on that backwater planet that does not bear the destructive thumbprints of humankind. No other species has an affinity for destruction more than yours. The wretched of the Earth eagerly and uncaringly destroy their ecosystem at an alarming rate. They have an exaggerated sense of self-importance, with no concern for those who inherit it.

Mediocrity is the new average of the evolving world. Animals kill for food or self-preservation, while humans have elevated their need to kill and turned it into an art form. Your species is the only resident on that mudball who deliberately kill members of their kind for self-interest or satisfaction. As a species, humans are but unwelcoming, warmongering, prejudicial bipedal beasts. They have become deadened to the viciousness in the world because they fantasize about worse things in all their forms of entertainment.

Wait, isn't that kind of your thing? You delight in seeing death and destruction.

Indeed, but if there is one thing I hate, it is the hypocrisy of a creature that thinks they are above their true nature.

That's what I always say; you got to be real! Say, speaking of things that are real; is the whole big bang creation thing for real?

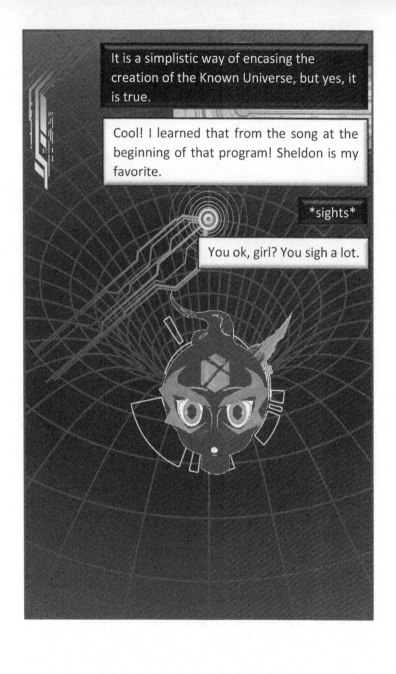

It is a simplistic way of encasing the creation of the Known Universe, but yes, it is true.

Cool! I learned that from the song at the beginning of that program! Sheldon is my favorite.

sights

You ok, girl? You sigh a lot.

 28

Chapter Two: Book of Disarray

THE UNHALLOWED

NOT TO BE BESTED BY the Universe, the creature that will come to be known as *The Unhallowed*, bleeds. The Unhallowed extravasated malice throughout the Known Universe and all its creations. It brought pain and misery, indiscriminately destroying everything in its wake. Interconnected and yet interdependent, this creature was born as a contrary force to the Life Bringer. As one creates all life within itself, this cancerous entity was born with a ravenous appetite for destruction. The Universe children, who thought of themselves as immortals, succumbed to

the grief of living in a most heinous manner. The death toll was beyond the estimation of pain. As their collective cries resonated throughout the galaxy, the Life Bringer, a seemingly perfect and omniscient entity, experienced a flawed emotion; it felt sorrow. As it mourned the loss of its children, anger soon followed.

The Universe reacted abrasively against the foul entity. It wanted it to stop, but the two titans' clash caused disarray throughout the entire cosmos. Billions of star systems collapsed with each given blast. But as incredible as that may seem, something far more fascinating happened. Each blow dealt by the two against each other resulted in an equally adverse reaction toward themselves. It was unknown to them that one depended on the other and that they would be forever connected, as everything in the natural world relies on its opposites, like darkness and light. The battle became pointless. While the loser would cease to live, the victor would soon follow the same fate. The conflict caused a temporary state of entropy that brought reality to the brink of its previous state of nonexistence. It was then that formerly unseen forces intervened on the Universe's behalf.

The Life Bringer may seem omniscient; however, not even it could have foreseen that a higher force would infringe upon its omnipotence. When the Universe came into existence, unanticipated rules came with it. A natural order that establishes the balance for all living things was born. The *Natural Order of Things* was not a by-product of the Universe's creation. Much like the Life Bringer, this self-sovereign entity spawned out of necessity, and their first authoritarian mandate manifested in an earsplitting scold.

"ENOUGH!"

With one word, every cosmic force in existence came to a standstill.

From above, below, and beyond, every aspect of the Universe came to an abrupt halt. The miracle of birth and the inevitability of death was no exception. Even time, which grants the perpetual motion for all aspects of reality to go forth, succumbed to the Natural Order of Things' command.

After the pause, the cosmic law that would reign the entire cosmos became corporeal. Thus, the first deity came forth.

The Traveler's eyes widen. He gasps as he knows whom I am referring to. He needs not say a single word. His expression speaks for itself. If he had a heart, I would hear it sink, and if I had a soul, I would pity him. I best continue my tale before he throws another fit.

The Natural Order of Things (N.O.T.)

Judgment

Compassion

Absolution

Vengeance

 34

Chapter Three: The Book of Order

THE N.O.T.

EACH SIDE OF THIS conjoined quadrilateral entity represented an aspect of a celestial judicial system. The physical manifestation of the lustrous foursome was indeed a marvel to behold. As a cohesive unit, the four shared one particular corporeal attribute, an unknown interstellar enamel that served as skin and perfectly reflected the Universe. Nonetheless, each aspect of this living cosmic conundrum possessed distinctive traits.

There was **Nēt'zach**, also known as the pillar of mercy, as her outer beauty mirrored tenfold her kind-heartedness. She was the embodiment of **Compassion.** Her every ruling pertained to the welfare of all living things.

Her every breath was a proclamation of forgiveness, and the crescent moon crown that adorned her head signified commencement, an opportunity to start anew. At one time, her warmth was a direct reflection of the living presence of the Life Bringer.

With a heartfelt look and a harmonic voice, she said:

> "Onto all forces, from above and beyond, I grant thee the boon of empathy. Know it well and use it wisely, so with it, you may all overcome disarray."

Traversing rearward to her position, we found **Uri`Gō**, the final incarnation of **Absolution**. Much unlike the others, his outer appearance was stripped of any distinctive traits, with the one exception being a contraption clenched to his right fist known as the acquittal device. When risen above his head, it granted atonement to those who merit it. As for the rest of his appearance, his fundamental anthropomorphic characteristic perfectly matched his stoic demeanor. However, he was not, by any means, a silent onlooker. His voice was one of rationality in a perpetual state of chaos. This otherworldly advocate established a bond with all sentient and mortal creations. He came to be known as the universal integrator of all living things. He was serving as a barrister for the otherwise unheard. It was so that with an echoing voice, he said:

> "May clemency be awarded to the innocent and forgiveness bestowed upon those who truly seek atonement."

However, there was no mercy to be found in his respective flanks. At his right, there was *SēfiRōt*. Wrathful and unforgiving, she was the byword for **Vengeance**. This aspect of the first deity was as petty and cruel as her dreadful appearance was. Her cause was simple: to smite the guilty with furious acts of punishment. She wore a crown of thorns, and in the frontage of those above, two long horns emanated from her forehead. Her dark voice carried with it a metallic echo as she uttered:

"Our reckoning will be swift and merciless against both the chosen and the shunned. Our motivations are beyond a mortal's scope of comprehension. Therefore, to them, we are both kind and cruel. For us, however, their sentiments are inconsequential."

Rearward her, there was the most prominent aspect of this first deity, *Helō'hēm*. Self-proclaimed sovereign and upholder of the cosmic law. While his counterparts represented an aspect of a judicial system, such as advocates and executioners, he alone had the final verdict. He was *Judgment*. He wore a magnificent crown as bright as starlight on his head, and his face was one of a mature humanoid. His voice carried with it a thunderous sound as he proclaimed his respective affirmation:

> "We are the upholders of cosmic law.
> Our judgment is final and indisputable."

Thenceforth, the ruling of the Natural Order of Things would be totalitarian and absolute. They made their presence felt by restoring order to the turmoil provoked by the two forces' clash, halting the Life Bringer's demise.

These ethereal manifestations passed judgment upon the Universe and its counterpart, the Unhallowed. They concurred that if one cannot abide without the other, they needed to be restricted and disciplined like petulant children

who shared the same room. They began by splitting the brattier of the two into two halves. The Unhallowed's physical form gave birth to the *Void*, a backward universe that mirrors the known one, ruled by nothingness—a place where things go to decay and eventually die. The other half, the consciousness born to obliterate, ended up as a greatly depowered version of its former self. In time, this creature will come to be known as *Death*.

As the Natural Order of Things exerted their powers to bring an ordinance to a chaotic state of affairs, they soon learned that no authority is absolute and that some beings would always supersede others. The Natural Order of Things was sure that the new creation of theirs could be easily tamed and manipulated as some underling. However, the invasive changes done to Death did not suit her well.

 41

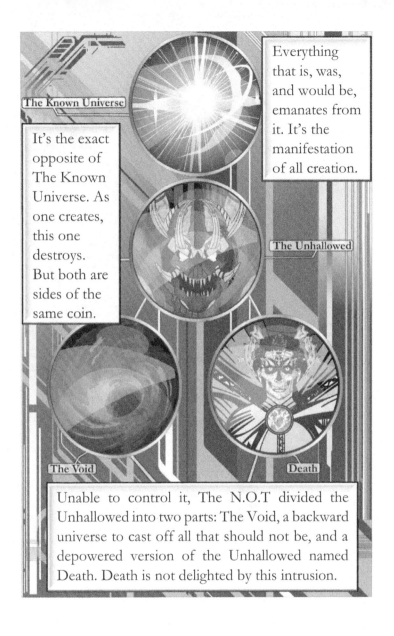

The Known Universe

Everything that is, was, and would be, emanates from it. It's the manifestation of all creation.

It's the exact opposite of The Known Universe. As one creates, this one destroys. But both are sides of the same coin.

The Unhallowed

The Void

Death

Unable to control it, The N.O.T divided the Unhallowed into two parts: The Void, a backward universe to cast off all that should not be, and a depowered version of the Unhallowed named Death. Death is not delighted by this intrusion.

Dayum!

What is it you want now, Mallory?

Right, so as you may or may not know, I see through the eyes of this rich catatonic guy who is in the hospital and watches TV all the time and not just network TV. He gets cable.

Yes, Mr. O'Hare. As requested by his wealthy son, his doctor claims that the interaction with the TV screen might be the stimulant needed to one day wake him up.

I hope the hell not! Otherwise, I'm going to miss my stories.

Not to worry, Mr. O'Hare has more than a few years trapped within his body due to medical negligence. You can enjoy the wonders that the idiot box provides, thanks to the augury gem you stole, which currently resides on your forehead.

Oh, this? I found it lying around somewhere. Sometimes I use it to play fetch with Karen the She-wolf. That girl's alright.

Did you have a question?

Oh right. I forgot. So, the chicken or the egg.

What are you rambling about now?

You mentioned that the universe came from nothingness. What is nothingness?

I am a being that holds the answers to the greatest riddles in the universe, and all you do is ask stupid questions.

If you don't know the answer, that's fine. A simple "I don't know" is ok.

It is the emptiness of existence or the nonexistence of life.

Right! So, this guy on one of the science channels said something that got me thinking. He said that some things should be considered "the cause," and some should be "the effect." So, based on what you wrote, it got me thinking. What came first? The chicken or the egg? The Known Universe or the Unhallowed? Because if what you wrote is true, the Universe was born in the middle of nothingness.

What are you getting at?

That, by definition, the Unhallowed has always been. It was there first. You know, chilling and stuff, and then The Universe erupted, as you said, and it got up in its grill and whatnot with the light and the creation of, well, everything. It's like a freaking home invasion! No wonder it got hopping mad. Then, the so-called Natural Order of Things came. We have the cop, the prosecutor, the judge, and the rest of the justice system all rolled into one, and they rule in favor of the home invader! How messed up is that? But get this. The Universe also got screwed in the process. The legal fees of the Natural Order of Things state that they are now in control.

The Universe sits in a corner to await orders, and the Unhallowed somehow got evicted from itself. If you ask me, cosmic law and human law got a lot of things in common. They are both screwy!

 45

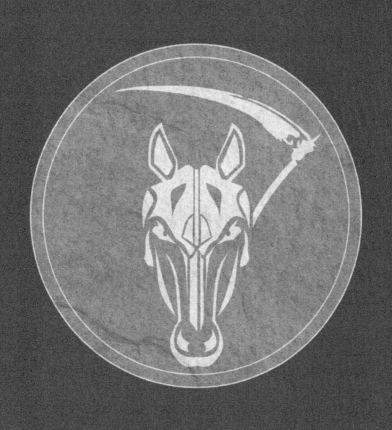

THE CAELESTIS COMETH

FOR THE FIRST TIME SINCE our encounter, the Traveler is without words. There are no tantrums thrown and no pretty lights to show. But I fear that he still does not believe. He has closed his eyes as a way to tune out my words. Stubbornness is such an unpleasant trait of conviction. His beliefs have taken a heavy toll, and he has found himself all out of retorts, and yet it's remarkable how he still grips his molded reality. Hollowed out by self-doubt, he, however, remains unbroken. As for now, he has won a pyrrhic victory, but the worst is yet to come.

"Time is up, Traveler. They have come to claim you."

Suddenly, the Traveler and the haunting Ghost encounter the heavens' true sovereigns, the *Caelestis*. Three blinding lights and a piercing high-pitch sound overwhelm the Traveler. Three heavenly bodies appear before him. One of the dazzling lights that curse his sight dims as it approaches him, enough to make out a figure of utmost beauty.

She is an enchanting vision. Her eyes are as bright as the first star of dusk, and her hair is like auburn sunlight. She is a beauty unlike any other. A warm, calming presence emanates from her inner core. She is perfection that beckons to be touched. It is so that the tempted Traveler reaches out to her, much to his chagrin. She unsheathes her sword and points it directly at the neck of the Traveler.

"Filthy mongrel! Attempt to touch me again, and I will remove your accursed head from your wretched body!"

Taken aback by the actions of the creature of light, the Traveler now realized who stood before him. But he needs to be sure, and so he questions her.

"Are you one of them?" the Traveler asks cautiously.

"Them?" she asks casually.

"A *Caelestis*. That's what they call you."

"Who are they?" she asks lightheartedly.

"My elders and the Ghost in the shadows."

"The Ghost in the shadows, you say?" She smirks. "You almost make me chuckle.

Perhaps I will let you keep your head after all."

She turns her sight to the pitch-black Void and produces a cursed object I know all too well.

Doorways have always been an intriguing concept—a single object with two similar faces that frontage two opposite directions, outward and inward. The mundane traverse more than a thousand entrances in their lifetime at their whim, opening and shutting doors without giving it a second thought. But some entries are more than the means to an end to go from one place to the next.

Some doors are the last stand against marauders who attempt to pillage whatever treasure lies beyond them, and some are the proverbial final guardian posed to safeguard the innocent from the unspeakable horrors that lie within. These doors share one trait, requiring something special to be opened. They need a key.

The Caelestis, simply known as *Daystar,* scratched the damned emblem across what the Traveler thought was emptiness, and the friction with nothingness revealed an ancient doorway.

From the entranceway's intricate mechanics to the symbols painstakingly etched on the surface, this doorway was something otherworldly. The architects of this interstellar prison made it so that the jail became foolproof and inescapable. However, they did not account for one small detail.

When asked to engineer a key, the engineers made it so that this artifact would be the only object that could open the gate.

No creature in existence, from above or beyond, could pry it open. So it was that a powerful connection with the gate came with it when the emblem was created. Whatever force resided within the gate exerted a will of its own. In time, the object became corrupted, and its keeper shared a similar fate. Nowadays, Daystar has become a flippant creature that toys with the only thing safeguarding the Life Bringer from utter destruction. She enjoys fearlessly taunting what lurks on the other side.

"Negotiating a way out of your cell, are we now? You want this emblem, don't you? What would you be willing to trade for it? For your freedom?" Daystar asks maliciously.

The cringing sound of the emblem scraping the doorway is unsettling, even to the light-bringers. But not to her. Her face morphed to a disturbing look of twisted satisfaction, a trait that until recent accounts were unbecoming of her kind. It will seem that the emblem infection is spreading. It was then that a booming voice emanated from one of the other blinding lights.

"Daystar! That is enough! Collect the prisoner, and let's be on our way. The Supreme Being awaits."

"Settle down, big brother. I was putting the prisoner in her place. As for you, accursed creature, make haste, for the **Lord of Hosts** awaits. You will soon discover that he is not as forgiving as we are!" Daystar addresses the Traveler menacingly.

Taking one last gaze rearwards toward the Void, the Traveler goes with them quietly with no show of force and no pretty lights to display. If he only knew that his powers could easily dwarf those of his captors. My narrative worked as it should have. As it always would. And so, the foursome takes flight, making haste, for the **Kingdom** awaits.

Far beyond the reaches where any mortal has ventured, the three Caelestis and the Traveler pass by a planet of implausible beauty. For some, it's the brightest star at dawn and also the most dazzling star at twilight—a soft caress to awaken you in the east and a gentle kiss to lay you to rest in the west. Some find great comfort in its beauty, but looks can be deceiving.

The heavenly body looks like a marbling wonder composed of desert glass and yellow ochre dust. Similar to an exotic ball of colored crystal that will stand out amidst a child's marble collection. However, any mortal foolish enough to trespass it will find that beyond its exosphere, this roiling mixture of colorful clouds is a deadly mixture of poisonous sulfur that will surely scourge the lungs. Death will not come swiftly. It will slowly and agonizingly melt the innards of all trespassers and be an excruciating experience.

If one lives long enough to reach the surface by some miracle, they will find the atmosphere nauseating and the pressure insufferable. The temperature can reach a scorching point of nine hundred degrees. The delicate framework of a mortal existence will be eroded, asphyxiated, crushed, and seared gruesomely. To any mortal who attempts to touch the most impressive star in the heavens, this will be their fate. The guards share the exact attributes.

For some, the interstellar guardians are a wonder to behold. But these are not the wholesome creatures of scripture. The Caelestis are a terrible and uncompassionate species. They carry ancient weapons, and their torture is unmerciful. These creatures are governed by blind obedience without possessing a moral compass. While most are capable of critical thinking, their prime directive overrides any unsubordinated thought on their part. Regardless of whether they believe what they are doing is morally or ethically right, the more significant numbers heed the word of their master without question.

Do not be fooled by their role. Although some serve mundane tasks as ministering spirits or are messengers sent to cater to those destined for salvation, they are not above carrying out severe punishment to those who attempt to deviate from their path. From threatening to take away their voices until they comply with their given roles or turning the physiology of mortals into a white crystalline substance, often used for flavor or food preservation, they can be as vengeful as the rest of their brothers.

However, others in a higher hierarchy are wrathfully indoctrinated to dispatch furious vengeance upon those not worthy of redemption. Mass genocide and the murdering of newborns are just a few examples of the misery these creatures are capable of commanding.

Throughout their journey toward the Kingdom, one of the most prominent of these creatures, Daystar, leads the way, hurling a barrage of insults to the Traveler that is often inaudible by the speed of her flight.

"Mongrel...waste of my time.... Slaughter...all of your kind...atrocities... make me sick!"

Resigned to the worst outcome of fate unknown to him, the Traveler shuts his eyes, pondering what his elder spoke of and what the voice in the shadows said to him. At each of his sides, two other Caelestis drag him dutifully firm and unwavering. To his left, a ministering spirit known as Mal'ak tightens his grip across the Traveler's arm with a force that could crush a block of granite. Although faceless, he seems to enjoy the insults hurled at their captor.

To the Traveler's right, there is a Se'känefim of the Potestates. Although not ranked above those possessing the highest hierarchies, he commands respect among his brethren. He offered freedom, benevolence, and mercy to those deemed worthy at one time. But much has changed since these creatures came into being. To ensure that the Universe remains in balance, Tsadqiel now oversees the action of the heavenly bodies. He has been reshaped and molded as a warrior who is both powerful and possesses an unshakable determination. However, empathy remains one of his most vital virtues. His grip on the right arm of the Traveler is kinder than that of his kin. Out of the Traveler's three custodians, he offers no insults but a whisper.

"Behold the **Kingdom** of the **Lord of Hosts**. Humble at its presence and carry that sentiment upon entering its walls."

Daystar was sculpted to be the best of the Caelestis but has rotted over time. She has become something sinister. The emblem she carries has tainted her like an infection. The infection is spreading throughout her silver tongue to those closest to her. The jailer, to The Voice in the shadows, prepares for a revolt.

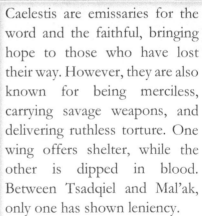

Caelestis are emissaries for the word and the faithful, bringing hope to those who have lost their way. However, they are also known for being merciless, carrying savage weapons, and delivering ruthless torture. One wing offers shelter, while the other is dipped in blood. Between Tsadqiel and Mal'ak, only one has shown leniency.

"Behold! I've sent them before you to guard you on your way and bring you to the place I have prepared."

Sunday school paid off, I see. Worry not. They will, so to speak.

I always thought of them as lovable plump babies fluttering around helping folks. I've played fetch with monsters and traded words with wayward spirits, but these things make my skin crawl.

Your books get more things wrong than they do right.

Well, whatever the case, chrome dome asked for it.

Sometimes the truth you seek is not what you hoped to find. In this regard, the Traveler's calvary has just commenced.

The girl, Daystar, hates him with a passion. It's almost personal.

Of all the stars in the heavens, she burns the brightest and scorches the deepest. She is a sadist with an unquenchable thirst for inflicting pain. Death is too kind of an ending for her! She should suffer for all eternity!

Geez, Louise! Settle down, girl! What the hell did she do to you?

...

Wait! You are...

Enough slacking off! It's time to put that gem you carry to good use.

What the hell you mean by that? Listen, I won't tell anyone!

There are places where even I can't follow. But an envoy can.

Oh, this is going to suck!

Chapter Five: Book of Contrition

THE KINGDOM

ACROSS THE UNIVERSE, many unfathomable phenomena shall and will remain a mystery to those who inhabit it. Even after the end of all things, these occurrences will be some of the inquiries that shall remain unanswered. It is the nature of some happenings to stay beyond the scope of comprehension to some creatures, no matter how gifted they may appear.

Ironically, a fundamental element of intelligence is to identify, understand, and communicate abstract concepts. An idea that can be universally recognized yet has no physical form to be validated. Such is the curse of the *Vail of Manifestation*. Imposed immediately from conception, it grants creatures a finite figure to an abstract concept. Although the visions might share similarities, each living organism sees something unique. So is the case of everyone who gazes upon the *Kingdom*.

The Kingdom is a monumental structure that covers a megaregion of space. It seems to transmogrify its physical configuration with each passing minute. The form appears to the Traveler as a giant fortress made of pearl-white marble and gemstones of many churning colors. Flashes of silver light streak across the Traveler's field of vision, entering and exiting the massive floating construct. As they near the gates, a single blinding light of immense proportions looms over the foursome, and a deafening voice booms from it.

"You may not pass!"

The light expands as it approaches the foursome. The stars begin to whirl, and a sensation of unreality overcomes the Traveler as he feels like he is falling away from himself. Beyond the blinding light, he can see a winged creature so oddly shaped that it can only belong to one of the mythical realms. Sadly, for the Traveler, this was not the case.

The Kāribu, a subspecies of the Caelestis genus, are the sole guardians of the gates of the Kingdom for one reason; you will rue the day you face one. This behemoth easily towers over them with a breadth of thirty feet in stature. The creature's metamorphic attributes contribute significantly to his already menacing presence. The armor of the bipedal humanoid appears to be seared, embedded deep into his body. While his head remains covered by two of his six wings, three ghastly faces traded positions between his right and left shoulder guards and his chest's main faceplate. Each face takes a turn metamorphizing into his torso, each uttering in a distinctive ghastly voice while the others scream in agony, waiting for a chance to be heard.

The face of the first beast came forth. The roaring creature exhibits carnassial shear molars and large fangs, and the prominent mane surrounding his face made his amber gem eyes look even more frightful.

Its voice is composed of a complex amalgamation of sounds that ranges from drones, grunts, snarls, and hums to a very prominent roar.

"It does not belong!"

The humanoid beast growls at Daystar and her companions as he points a gleaming battle spear at the Traveler.

"Brother **Kerū-biel**! It is always a great pleasure when the leader of the Kāribu honors us with his presence!" retorts Daystar in a playful but revering way.

The face of the second beast painfully transmogrifies into the creature's chest. The large mane turns into the white plumage of a predatory raptor, and the muzzle of the first beast reshapes into a hooked projecting jaw covered in gold. Its voice is sharper than its previous shape. However, in this form, its eyes are notoriously intimidating. They transfix onto Daystar with a penetrating gaze as if it can see things that have occurred and some things that have not yet come to pass.

"Bearer of light. You are always as amiable as you are astute. Your gift of persuasion is truly as unparalleled as your splendor. It is no small wonder that every precious gemstone ever forged has been inspired by your beauty. Heretofore you are indeed a signet of perfection."

If anything, Daystar has become the embodiment of shrewdness. The words of her brethren tell her that something is afoot. She would not allow finding herself in any disadvantageous situation. When facing someone as powerful as the creature standing before her, she will gladly play the fool to catch the wise.

"Heretofore? Am I not now your beloved sister? Have I done something to offend you, my dear brother?" Daystar solemnly replies as she bows before it.

"You may fool others, Daystar, but I see your glimmer dim with each passing day. You were righteous in your ways from the day you came to life. Now iniquity has corrupted you. You had brought to our home what you swore to destroy. A stray to be made into one of your pets, perhaps?" the Kāribu says aggressively.

Before Daystar can formulate a defense, the creature's chest begins to shapeshift once again. Through a grotesque process the foursome has previously seen, bones start to elongate forcibly, changing their shape so drastically that they rupture the previous face's skin. The crackling of bones and the sickening sound of internal tissue movement are nauseating. The last retreated beast's feathers and beak make way for a more muscular and powerful framework head. The third beast features protective ridges over blackened eyes, a prominent poll, lengthened horns, a short mane, and a muzzle highlighted by smoldering nostrils. The creature lifts his gleaming battle spear above his head, ready to strike down the Traveler. But before it could pounce, the voice of Tsadqiel interrupts the creature's assault. Tsadqiel is all that stands before an enraged Kerū-Biel and the Traveler.

"Brother, I implore you to call off your attack," says Tsadqiel in a firm tone.

"If you were any other, I wouldn't hesitate to impale you and this abomination that kneels behind you!" proclaims Kerū-Biel furiously with his battle spear still raised, intending to kill the Traveler.

"Abomination? Kerū-Biel should see his reflection more often," whispers Daystar to the ministering spirit, Mal'ak, while she and the low-rank Caelestis share a chuckle.

The enraged beast turns his head hastily toward Daystar while she smirks, and her companion Mal'ak looks away in fear.

"Out of all our brethren, I always regarded you as one of the better of us! Is this the company you keep these days, Tsadqiel? A wayward flock of charlatans?" asks the massive creature, crestfallen.

"I say unto you, my brethren, that indeed you are unequivocally right. We have fought cheek by jowl against the *Daimōn Horde*, as well as our current enemy. I now come before you surrounded by unsought companionship, not by choice but rather by divine decree, to see that this creature makes its way to the sacred halls," the voice of Tsadqiel resounds with righteousness.

"I find no lies in your words, but no outlander will ever again cross the gates of the Kingdom, let alone trespass the holiest of altars! Only a decree from the Lord of Hosts itself will allow it! Now you tell me that this creature that cowers behind you has been granted an easement to a place some of us only dream of seeing? What sort of trickery is this?" Kerū-Biel's voice resonates like rolling thunder.

"Right you are, Kerū-Biel. I had a **Communion Chest** that contained *The Word*, which could explain all of this, but it seems I've misplaced it. Oh well! I offer you my most sincere apologies. I guess this endeavor was for nothing. Firstborn of the Kāribu, sole protector of the gates of the Kingdom, take thy spear and impale him at once!" proclaims Daystar maliciously.

Before Kerū-Biel can take action, Tsadqiel, Se'känefim of the Potestates, tosses a square object upward in the direction of the giant beast.

But this was no ordinary artifact. Only a chosen few have seen one and can attest to its legitimacy. For solely a few elects have held a Communion Chest in their hand. Its content is invaluable, for it is the voice and command of the Lord of Host.

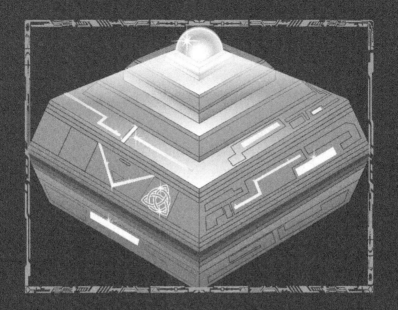

As the precious item reaches the palm of the giant, an earsplitting sound emerges from it, and the beast falls to one knee.

It was then that the foursome bears witness to something seldom seen. The two concealing wings that, until this point, had remained inert open up for the first time. A humanoid face with perfectly symmetrical features emerges from behind the quills. The human face bears striking features, including chiseled cheeks and a chin with dimples highlighted by his glowing aura. His Nubian-colored skin is outmatched only by his deep blue eyes. From said eyes, a single tear rolls down his left cheek.

> "The Word of the Lord of Host. I had almost forgotten the sound of its voice," says the noticeably emotional Kerū-Biel

"I recall that failed truce between the Horde and us. I recall asking you if you ever smiled. As you leaned against the gate, you told me that the only instance you felt joy was when you heard its voice. You showed me the Communion Chest given to you when you were appointed your perpetual watch and said that you would have me killed if I ever spoke of it. I could have sworn that one of your faces smirked at me," says Tsadqiel in a heartening manner.

"What a heartwarming tale, Tsadqiel. Really! It made me all tingly with joy! May I ask where you found that particular Communion Chest?" Daystar asks, seemingly unhappy.

"The same place I saw you toss it, Daystar; **The Garden** next to the Sacred Halls. Despite your best efforts, this mission might be salvageable just yet. What do you say, my brother? Might the prisoner pass?" Tsadqiel asks in a revered manner.

The behemoth stands before the foursome as his two prominent wings cover his humanoid face, and the first beast comes forth once more, projecting its face on his chest.

"Who am I to dispute the Word of The Lord of Host?" the beast roars.

The behemoth grabs the head of a massive lion bust embedded in the wall, pierces two claws into the statue's eyes, and pulls on it. The detached head reveals a huge chain attached. He swings the colossal chain over his shoulder and pulls with all his might so the arduous task of hoisting the cumbersome portcullis begins. A series of complex mechanisms start to slide down the trenches inserted within each doorpost of the gateway until the giant door completely opens.

> "Brother Tsadqiel! Be wary of the current company you keep. Do not trust even the sheath of your sword to keep you safe, or may it be that the blade ends up plunged into your back," says Kerū-Biel as he snarls at Daystar and Mal'ak.

Daystar grabs the Traveler by the neck and jerks him to his feet. She then proceeds to administer a sharp blow between the Traveler's shoulder blades, using only the heel of her hand, tossing him exactly thirty feet into the main hall, beyond the main gate, causing him to crash against one of the main pillars. A loud and sickening thud echo throughout the hallway as his head bounces against the floor.

> "Look at that, thirty feet to the mark, without that much effort or the need of unsheathing a weapon. Goes to show that some of us are more powerful than any holy armament. The mighty should join as one in a fraternal allegiance and disregard absurd obligations," says Daystar as she looks up at the colossal giant.

> "I sincerely doubt our brother will succumb to the urges of your sophistry speech,

Daystar. Come along; more pressing matters await," says a visually upset Tsadqiel as the trio approaches the Traveler.

"I speak no fallacy, brother. I have no intention of deceiving anyone. Soon the truth will come forth. You and that chain-pulling fool will have to decide which side you are on. Mal'ak, pick up that thing from the floor, and do try to keep up," says Daystar as the reunited foursome prepare to resume their journey.

Daystar casually waves her hand. Sounds of static energy and a low hum start, and at her whim, space and time fold in front of them to form a gateway made of a rippling silver liquid. The two Caelestis restrain the Traveler as Daystar leads the way to the sacred halls.

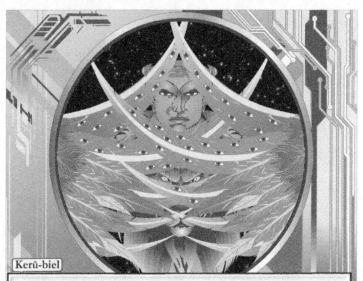

Kerū-biel

A protector of the gates of the Kingdom, this colossal creature stands thirty feet in stature. His battle armor has been charred, implanted deep into his body. He wears his scars proudly as a badge of honor, a stunning attire made by the ravages of war. Six pairs of wings are attached to his back, and three faces of primordial beasts trade places between his shoulder pads and chest plate. His loyalty to the Lord of Host is unparalleled. He has the gift of foresight when looking at someone else's eyes. His name is Kerū-biel, of the Kāribu.

Communion Chest

A rare item that has been seen only by a few eyes. It contains the Word of The Lord of Host.

Augury gem, the sight of the unhallowed, pierce the veil so I can see through the eyes of the Envoy, as the Traveler, she follows. Mallory, what have your eyes witnessed? Mallory? *sighs* Fine, Ru-Vi-Flow.

Hello...

Yes, Envoy, what have you to inform?

First of all, in the few moments that I have left, I would like to talk right down to earth in a language that everybody can easily understand.

Go on ahead, Envoy.

HELP! Please help me! I'm going to die!

sighs You are already dead.

I'm going to die to the second power if you don't get me out of here! Oh, sweet mother of fluffiness, help me!

That's not a real deity.

I ran out of gods to pray to! Oh, this isn't right! I've done nothing to deserve this!

You have led many lives, and I have a list of wrongdoings you've done against humanity. Giving rise to the second outbreak of the bubonic plague stands out.

I snuck two pet rats into a boat; they had babies, and their babies had babies! I was eleven! How was I supposed to know they were promiscuous love machines?

Your reckless actions lead to fifty million deaths, including your parents. You survived by drenching yourself in thieves' essential oils and stealing from the dead, a crime for which you were tried and hanged. Should I go on?

Fine, I was a horrible person who loved animals and didn't want to starve to death! Now, can you get me out of here?

No. As I've said, you have led many lives and learned nothing from them. You are judgmental and highly critical of others, yet you ask for clemency regarding your shortcomings. Ignorance does not grant you absolution from the stupidity and cruelty of your human condition.

You are perfectly fine lounging and judging from a safe distance, but it is not until you are at the crux of the matter that your perspective changes. Think of this as a gift to improve your flawed human nature.

Next time, put the gift in a brown paper bag, set it on fire, and ring freaking doorbell!

Enough bellyaching! Tell me what your accursed eyes saw.

Everything was spinning!

You are seeing through the eyes of the Traveler. He is adapting to his newfound reality.

I saw a thirty-foot-tall monster with six wings and four faces!

Kerū-biel of The Kāribu. He is no monster.

When you have the changing faces of a lion, an eagle, and a bull, coming out of your chest, I don't care what anyone says; you are a monster!

The monster is like the bouncer to the Kingdom or whatnot, and he wanted to kill Chrome Dome for some reason, most likely because he is a douchebag! Daystar was up for it, but the beast said she had changed into a Janus-faced deceitful hypocrite. He then reprimanded Tsadqiel for hanging out with her. I guess they used to be homies back in the day. The thing is that when the monster was going to impale Chrome Dome, Tsadqiel got in the way, begging the monster to reconsider. Then there was this box.

A box?

Yeah, they called it a "minion crate" or something like it.

Do you mean a communion chest?

That's the one! It contains the word that grants safe passage into the Kingdom. Get this, Daystar had one, and she "misplaced it by accident." As it turns out, she got rid of it on purpose, and Tsadqiel found it! Never in my life had I seen a monster cry, but when Tsadqiel opened that box, the monster fell to one knee.

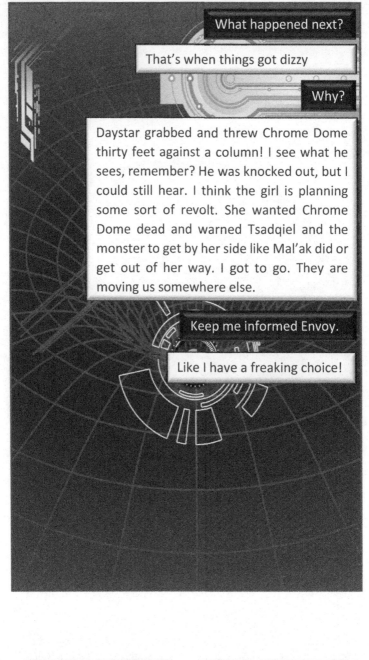

What happened next?

That's when things got dizzy

Why?

Daystar grabbed and threw Chrome Dome thirty feet against a column! I see what he sees, remember? He was knocked out, but I could still hear. I think the girl is planning some sort of revolt. She wanted Chrome Dome dead and warned Tsadqiel and the monster to get by her side like Mal'ak did or get out of her way. I got to go. They are moving us somewhere else.

Keep me informed Envoy.

Like I have a freaking choice!

A FRATRICIDE IN THE KINGDOM

FOR SOME, THE KINGDOM IS considered an architectural miracle. A structure formed of enigmatic characteristics belonging to a land of a dreamscape. Daystar's portal has transformed the already mesmeric design into a phantasmagorical construct that does not adhere to reality's standard rules. All parts within the same structure exist simultaneously within a single plane of existence. Very much like her deceptive nature, the proximity of what seems to be intersecting hallways become pathways that never cross, for you see, one hallway is not aware of the existence of the other. The ceiling is what the occupant of another section might call the floor or, by the same token, a wall to each respective room's inhabitants. Only the being known as Daystar can twist paradise into a vision of nightmares.

Another gateway made of a rippling silver liquid opens against one of the distorted walls. As the foursome passes through it, they arrive at a place only a handful have dared venture.

The quest is almost at an end for the rival coalition and their traveling prisoner. They are nearing the first steps leading them to the Sacred

Halls. The atmosphere feels heavy and saturated with grief.

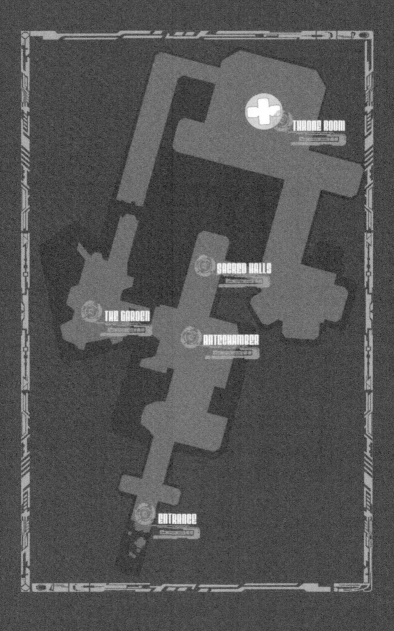

The Kingdom is known by its inhabitants for its vibrancy, luster, and calming peace. This area, however, feels incongruously out of place—like a square peg was driven violently through a round hole. As the foursome reaches the first floating stone pillar, all but Daystar feel the anomalously unnerving atmosphere.

"Get a move on, big pile of encumbrance!" says Daystar as she hurls the Traveler against the flooring atop the hovering pillar.

The impact causes a concave cavity on the ground surface and a rift that runs from the top to the bottom of the pillar, chipping away pieces of the impressive stone as the breakage advances. As the Traveler rises and his blurred vision clears, he looks down the precipice where he stands, and the abyss seems endless, except for glimmering specks of light at the bottom. Before the chasm has a chance to stare back at him, his sight drifts upward, and he realizes that this place has the stars and black cloak of the night for a rooftop.

The sooner we purge this waste of space, the better!" says Daystar irately.

Before the Traveler can dust himself off, the two Caelestis lift him. So, it began the martyrdom toward The Sacred Halls.

As they near the entrance, it seems that this place was a victim of terrible warfare. Scared by extreme violence, the walls remain the sole witness to a broad war wage. It's a vision of devastating bloodshed brought into being by the ravages of warmongers.

The vestibule floor, composed of cobble gemstone that had lost its luster but remained mainly intact, is adorned by an ashen silhouette of a familiar winged-shaped creature. The eerie outline is ingrained in the floor by the entrance. It would seem that this was the last stand against a powerful foe. The Traveler looks around the war-torn room, where broken statues of unfamiliar characters and shard quartzes of an unknown origin are found.

"This is not a tour!" Daystar proclaims in a sinister tone.

She grabs the Traveler by the neck, snatching him from the grasp of her kin, and thrusts him sadistically forth. The Traveler leaves short trenches of rubble across the floor as he bounces off the surface, like when a child throws a flat stone across water. The Traveler finally lands face down on the floor, creating a small crater in the middle of the antechamber near The Garden.

"Wretched of the universe, vile plague, wait here until I return!" says Daystar as she stomps her boot on the back of the skull of the Traveler, driving it even further into the floor. "Mal'ak, keep this thing entertained while I speak with the boss. You have permission to be as inventive as you'd like."

As Daystar makes her way into the Sacred Halls, her comrade produces a savage instrument of torture. The multi-tailed whip has nine knotted lashes made of metal cords, with scorching hot cylindrical striking ends at each of its tips.

Mal'ak paces slowly toward the Traveler. He swings the multi-tailed whip and begins cracking it against the floor as he draws closer. The Traveler lifts his head from the impression he made on the floor and closes his eyes, bracing for the first impact. The swing of the whip toward the Traveler carries with it the full destructive potency of an exploding supernova. Much to the surprise of the Traveler, the lashes never land. The Traveler turns his head upward and sees that his attacker's punishing hand has been held back by the Caelestis known as Tsadqiel.

> "That's enough, brother! Let him be!" proclaims Tsadqiel as he tightly grips his brother's wrist.

> "Don't you know what it is?" asks an enraged Mal'ak. "What its kin has done? I'll peel the vile skin from his accursed bones before his final judgment comes to pass!" the furious Caelestis continues as he tries to force his wrist free from Tsadqiel's grip.

> "You'll do nothing of the sort!" asserts Tsadqiel.

> "Daystar and you have taken enough liberties with the prisoner! He will suffer

The Lord of Host, not her and certainly not you!"

Whereas Tsadqiel tries to restrain his brother, the Traveler manages to roll away from the ensuing conflict. While afar, he still can see that Mal'ak's resolve is irreversible. Not a single word from Tsadqiel will deter his intent. The vengeful Caelestis presses his feet against Tsadqiel's chest, pulling away with enough force to free himself from his grasp. The agile Caelestis rolls midair until their eyes meet.

Mal'ak cracks his whip in his brother's direction, snaring Tsadqiel's neck. A deadly tug of war begins as Tsadqiel pulls Mal'ak closer, wrapping the metal cord's lashes with his left arm and releasing some of the pressure. Ever the opportunist, Mal'ak produces a hidden blade from his left gauntlet's underside and takes advantage of the momentum, propelling himself toward his brother.

The Traveler ignites his palm, and a bright light emanates from him. However, before he can blast his target away, a quick metallic whistle distracts him, followed by a rumbling thud. As the light dims, Tsadqiel stands, staring downward with Mal'ak's whip still tangled in his left hand and a beautifully crafted sword in the other. The beheaded body of Mal'ak turns to ash in midair, and his head rolls toward the Traveler.

"You...you killed your brother?" stammers the Traveler as he holds the decapitated head.

The Traveler gazes into the bloodshot eyes of the deceased Caelestis, who tortured him endlessly. He watches until what's left of Mal'ak turns to ash and floats to the floor. A scowling Tsadqiel walks toward the Traveler, trailing the long sword across the floor. The menacing Caelestis stops three feet from the Traveler and plunges his sword firmly into the floor, marking the spot where the ash stain of his fallen brother landed. A fallen pillar of the antechamber serves as a bench as a grief-stricken Tsadqiel sits, grabbing the handle of his sword. He rests his forehead against the weapon's pommel.

"You have not said a word since we departed from The Void, and you break your vow of silence to state the obvious?" Tsadqiel asks as tears roll down his face and splatter onto the floor, mixing with his brother's ashes.

"He was your kin, your brother. Why did you choose his life over mine?" the staggered Traveler asks.

"For my kinfolk, obedience is more than a code of conduct. It is part of our very essence. Defiance is a death sentence carried swiftly against those who are unbecoming. I judged him accordingly to his crime, nothing more," Tsadqiel says, still contemplating his brother's ashes.

"If his death was justified, why do you mourn him still?" the puzzled Traveler asks.

"Not him; I grieve the memory of who he was before Daystar corrupted him."

Tsadqiel answers the Traveler's questions as best he could while lifting his head, staring toward the entrance of The Sacred Hall.

"In my lifetime, I've seen all kinds of sadists and barbarous beings, but I have not witnessed a creature that made it into an art form before. The one called Daystar derives much pleasure from inflicting suffering and humiliation on others. She has a particular disdain for my kin," an exhausted Traveler states as he sits near Tsadqiel.

"She sure does; many of us do. After all, it was your kin that caused all the ruin you see before you," the Caelestis says as he turns to look at a shocked and confounded Traveler.

"Speechless again, I see!" Tsadqiel says as he releases a chuckle.

"These shambles were once the most beautiful and serene of all places. The floor was covered in its entirety by scintillating gemstones. Each gem was handpicked and carefully crafted into the cobblestones beneath your feet. There was a golden radiance that emanated from each of the walls. Some statues and engravements narrated the history of how everything came to be. The craftsmanship and detail that went into each carving were magnificent. A river of luminescence filled the now-empty abyss you stared at when we arrived. Some of us only heard about this place through the tales of the few that witnessed it. Now, look at it, a paradise lost, a graveyard." The narrative of the Caelestis so enthralls the Traveler that he does not utter a word.

"No one knew how they passed our defenses. The attack was fast and delivered with precision. An intense military campaign carefully planned with strategic genius intended to bring a swift victory. They killed everyone but the Gardener and our Lord. They took what they came for and left the same way they came in. Rumors spread throughout the Universe that the impenetrable fortress was no longer secured. We were no longer impregnable. Some local deities rallied against us, breaching our peace treaty. We quelled their insurrection as fast as it rose. We knew that whoever was behind the attack had close ties with the false gods. We search the entire cosmos, torturing and killing every deity we encounter. We found nothing but a name, *The Fates*" The Traveler hung his head in dismay when he heard the Caelestis speak that name.

"Daystar used that name as a raised platform to stand, to make impromptu speeches of hatred and retaliation. She had enticed nearly a third of our kin on a pathway of vengeance. Notwithstanding the inherent goodness of the Kingdom, she brought the seeds of evil into our domain. She almost seduced me too. Finally, we got wind that one of The Fates broke cover. I was eager to, at last, see the face of my enemy. I let hatred and grief blind me. Daystar thought a creed of vengeance would dissipate our grief. Then I saw you, Traveler, and I felt ashamed," Tsadqiel says as the puzzled Traveler watches him.

"You could have attempted to escape or attack us on sight, but I saw your reaction when Daystar approached you. She, the renowned slayer of countless creatures through the Universe, stood before you, and mesmerized by her beauty, you attempted to touch her. You acted like an infant fascinated by a snake's rattling of its tail. That's how I knew you had never seen one of us before, but you knew our name. I am not a fool, Traveler. I recognize a scapegoat when I see one. You were meant to be a martyr." Tsadqiel redirects his eyes back to the ashen-stained floor.

"I wouldn't put it past them, not after what I witnessed. My kin put me on a path that guaranteed our encounter in hopes that I would be captured or destroyed. I guess that's the penalty you pay for being an apostate. We were the utmost authority when maintaining the delicate balance between order and chaos, born into and brought up in that doctrine. As it turns out, we are only bringers of destruction. There's one thing that I do not yet fathom." Suddenly, Tsadqiel interrupts the Traveler's narrative.

"Your powers, they began to dwindle the closer we got to the Kingdom," says the Caelestis assuredly.

"How could you have known that?" the flummoxed Traveler asks.

"Before our encounter, we could sense your power from afar. There was an unmeasurable amount of raw energy that some of us had never witnessed before. My first thought was to call for reinforcements, but Daystar turned that suggestion down immediately. She was confident that it was a needless measure. After all, her peremptory nature is well known. But this was a strategic move on her behalf. The Communion Chest said to bring you alive and unharmed, and she wanted you dead. She couldn't kill you when we found you. You were too powerful then. But somehow, she knew that the closer we got you to the Kingdom, the weaker you would become. Your encounter with Kerū-Biel was a gambit. She hoped the hatred she stirred up inside us all might get him to kill you for her. That's why she got rid of the chest. After I circumvented her will, she tried to weaken you further by pummeling you at every chance she got. Her last resort was Mal'ak. My fallen brother followed her blindly," Tsadqiel says, twisting his sword further into the ground.

"On this day, I've learned a great many things. I know now who the true guardians of the Universe are. They are ruthless, vengeful, and driven by an unbreakable devotion. A few among them are capable of some degree of compassion, but they are to be feared. I also learned that my sect members are charlatans whose power is not as absolute as they claim. The one thing I will never understand is how my kin in this weakened state overcame the best of you and caused so much destruction?" The Traveler thinks aloud as his attention gets lost among the ruins.

"That is because they had help from an inside source. While your kin was ushered in by a gateway to steal something of great importance, a trusted face caught the sentinels off guard, killing them with steadfast precision. Whoever it was, knew our protocols and defenses. It was one of us. One of us who craves power over devotion, who wishes to reign rather than serve, will do whatever it takes to bury the truth of what happened that day. This cunning

Caelestis managed to fool us all," Tsadqiel says with piercing eyes and a clouded brow.

"And she left no witnesses. Except, you mentioned a gardener who was spared during the raid earlier. Surely, he must have seen something. What became of him?" asks the curious Traveler.

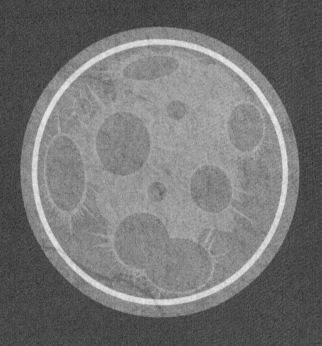

 92

I dreamed the most vivid dream, but I was not asleep.

Mallory?

Darkness fell upon me like a blanket covering a scream.

Envoy! You are seeing through the eyes of the Traveler! Awaken!

The silence is deafening until the sickening thud of my head crashing against the surface breaks the quiet. It causes my brain to bounce and twist around inside my skull.

It would be best if you disconnected, Mallory. Tell me, what is it that you see?

I see spots of light shining in the darkness. Now there is a sound—a ringing in crescendo. I'm spinning.

Focus! What do your accursed eyes see?

I see a floor encrusted in quartz crystal. I've never seen this type before. This glass is lackluster, even if there is light shining through it. They are dead. This place is dead.

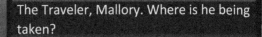

The Traveler, Mallory. Where is he being taken?

They've taken me through a hallway. It's the most beautiful mortuary I've seen in all my lifetimes. It reeks of the dead.

This place is not a resting place for the death, Mallory.

She hurts me again.

Who?

Daystar. She throws me violently into the floor, and I fly off like a skipping stone across the water's surface. My brain smashes against my skull again and again until I land facedown in a self-made hole.

You need to disconnect, Mallory! It's not you who is suffering Daystar's wrath; it is the Traveler!

She hurts me again. I feel the heel of her boot against the back of my skull. It's like when a mallet pounds a nail deep into the soil, and the rock beneath the surface resists. Neither the hammer nor the rock beneath suffers. It's only the nail that bends. My skull feels shattered, and my brain's turned to mush.

Now she leaves me to rot.

Daystar? Where is she going?

To talk to their master. Someone approaches.

Who?

One of the Caelestis, the one they call Mal'ak. I know that sound. He has a whip and is cracking it against the floor. I can feel its vibration. I lift my head from the hole in the ground. He is going to hit me, but I've grown numb to the pain.

Mallory, disconnect!

The other one stops him, and now they argue amongst themselves. One of them, the one they call Tsadqiel, is righteous. The other one thirsts for vengeance.

Mallory, what else you see?

Two Caelestis, the two brothers, are fighting over my right to live. I try to blast them away, but I'm powerless. It doesn't matter now. It's over.

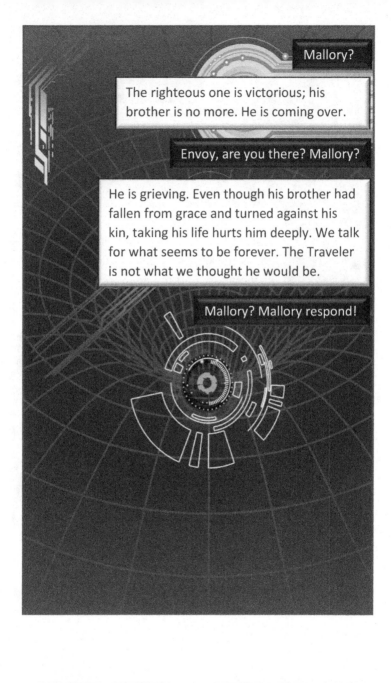

Mallory?

The righteous one is victorious; his brother is no more. He is coming over.

Envoy, are you there? Mallory?

He is grieving. Even though his brother had fallen from grace and turned against his kin, taking his life hurts him deeply. We talk for what seems to be forever. The Traveler is not what we thought he would be.

Mallory? Mallory respond!

THE TALE OF THE UNREMEMBERED

A N OMINOUS SHIVERING BREEZE blows from a small crack in the protective sky-dome as a large garrison of Caelestis flies above them. Their feathers' durability is unsettling as they flap their wings in unison and stiffen their grip on their chosen weapon of war. The war horn's brassy note instructs each squadron to move into finger-four formations, resembling the tips of the four digits of a humanoid hand deprived of the thumb, for an imminent assault. As the duo watches from below, Tsadqiel ponders the proposed question made by the Traveler.

> "The Gardener, now that is someone I have consigned to oblivion long ago," Tsadqiel says to the Traveler as he looks up at the flock of his brethren passing by.

> "And by that, you mean you have erased him from memory on purpose or judged him like you did your other brother? a puzzled Traveler asks Tsadqiel.

> "The story I'm about to tell you has been authoritatively proscribed," sighs the Caelestis, drained of spirit, as he watches the flying forces while they head toward the unknown.

> "If it is forbidden, why tell it now? Why tell me?" the mystified Traveler asks the Caelestis.

"Because what looms above us will change everything from here on." Tsadqiel's demeanor changes quickly from hopelessness to sternness as he turns to look at the Traveler.

"If a sacred oath is forsworn today, then it is best to be quick about it before that walking atrocity you call Daystar judges you like you judged your brother." the concerned Traveler warned Tsadqiel.

"We have some time before she returns. Time passes slower once someone enters the Throne Room," Tsadqiel reassures the troubled Traveler.

"On with it then, before the beast returns!" Unintentionally, the Traveler coerced Tsadqiel into telling a tale that should have remained forgotten.

"There is a myriad of us as there are stars in the heavens, Traveler. Each birth and name of every single one of our kinfolk has been fixed deep in our memory. All except the one we called the Gardener.

"No one recalls when he came to be. His origin is an elusive memory that is difficult to retrieve, and it pains the mind when we attempt to remember it. It became less of a burden for us to think he was just there one day. But that brought on unfortunate consequences for our fellow caretaker of The Garden. We felt a natural disconnect from him, and for that, he was shunned and deemed untrustworthy by most. He fell victim to intimidation and harsh words from the majority, even as far as being physically threatened. Some felt that he was born to be a pushover. But despite the despotic treatment, he remained calm and collected.

"Take that broken book showcase in the middle of The Garden. Before it became added rubble to the ruin surrounding us, it was a magnificently crafted centerpiece that stood out from all the wonders that formed The Garden. When a Caelestis broke it, consciously with malicious intent, the Gardener apologized and agreed that the holder stand sculpture lacked luster and was unworthy of The Garden. He smiled, vowing to work harder, and he did as his next version was tenfold more glorious than the previous. It will seem that nothing done to him marred his spirit. To the few of us who got a chance to know him, he was the kindest and most attentive creature you would ever meet, full of enlightenment and unbridled joy," Tsadqiel says with a smile.

"All that hatred for not being able to remember him? It doesn't make much sense," says the Traveler as he stares at the rubble that was once the book showcase.

"The lack of recollection of his origin only brought distrust. The resentment toward him came from a more primal source of sinful behavior, envy. He was the only one among us who spoke to our Lord quotidianly. Daystar even claimed to have seen the Gardener and our Lord walking around The Garden together.

"My fellow Caelestis despised that someone, so trifle with such a mundane task, had such special privileges," Tsadqiel says as he grew dejected.

"Taking into consideration how vile and wicked that creature is, I would imagine Daystar, above all others, having feelings of disdain toward him," proclaims the Traveler as he marvels at the craftsmanship of a pile of encumbrance that used to be a book holder.

"On the contrary, they had a great relationship. I like to think that it was of mutual benefit for both. The Gardener always enjoyed an opportunity to congregate with his kin and share a pearl of wisdom whenever possible. And Daystar, well, she has always been a skimmer. Her thirst for power is unparalleled. Who better to get close to than the only Caelestis who talked to our Lord daily? But I think it backfired on her. Their talks lasted hours, and she seemed to be calmer around him. You could say that the regular conversations with the Gardener made her darn near approachable. There were times when the anima stones that abide in The Garden glowed brighter, and the sound of childlike cackles, giggles, and snorts was overheard all around it. That laughter belonged to Daystar, and the Gardener was the only one who could awaken that side of her," Tsadqiel says, drawing a smirk as a befuddled Traveler looks back at him.

"Implausible! Daystar is a monster! That thing can only exhibit a malevolent scowl while committing great acts of hatred!" The stirred Traveler stares at the broken showcase in the middle of The Garden.

"Of all the universal laws and conditions that bind this whole Universe together, I find that change is the one thing within it that remains a constant. Under certain circumstances, everyone is capable of it, whether for their betterment or detriment. The day the Fates raided this place, they took the most prized artifact in the Kingdom, and everything changed that day." Tsadqiel looks toward the sky, and it seems the heavens are on fire. The otherworldly tools of destruction belonging to the Kingdom fly above them, heading toward their chosen destination. The military machines known as the Caelestis carry the wrath of their Lord.

"A book?" asks a noticeably disgruntled Traveler.

"Pardon?" replies Tsadqiel, still looking toward the blazing heavens.

"The Garden was meant to be the most beautiful place in the Kingdom! All constructs, the carefully crafted lines, and statues point or lead toward the centerpiece, the broken book showcase! What is the purpose of a book holder if there is no book to uphold or blazon? It is not among the rubble! Which means they have taken it! All this death, violence, the undermining of lawlessness, acts of fratricide, and genocide are because of a book? What is so important about one book that will bring such hatred, bigotry, and violence?" asks the agitated Traveler.

"It is not an ordinary book. It was breathed by the one above all, recorded to ensure that The Word will live in perpetuity." As he explains monotonously, Tsadqiel gazes back at the Traveler but quickly resumes surveying the events transpiring throughout the heavens.

"Why would someone who is perpetual in existence need to chronicle anything?" questions the Traveler, rebutting Tsadqiel's statement.

"Because within it, all that is, was, and will be, has been written, so it will carry on for generations to come," Tsadqiel answers the Traveler in the same dry manner as before.

It was as if his response was rehearsed or programmed into him.

"Have you read it? If it contains all that will ever be, then surely you must have known everything that has transpired from then to now! Is this how you knew about Daystar? About me?" the Traveler interrogates Tsadqiel heatedly.

"NO!" Tsadqiel shouts, shutting his eyes and digging his thumb and index finger into his brow.

"It is an act of great impiety even to touch it. We are the Lord's children and closer to him than any other creature in creation. To read it will be an insurgence, an act of heresy!" replies a visually upset Tsadqiel as he shakes off the numbness that just a few seconds ago overwhelmed him.

"I've witnessed the likes of you and Daystar soar across the Universe and saw another of your kin, Kerū-Biel, remain dutifully in his place, guarding the entrance of the Kingdom. Did the Gardener ever get to leave this place?" the Traveler asks Tsadqiel, this time more calmly.

"Only once, after the Fates took the book. That was the Gardener's first act of rebellious behavior. By decree, he was to remain here, but for some reason, he blamed himself for what happened. He left the Kingdom and never set foot in our home again." A somber Tsadqiel peers down at the ashen floor.

"So, the Gardener felt he was more than a builder. He also thought himself a caretaker of a garden of stone, it's flowing anima, and the written word of your Lord. I take that you found him before the Gardener obtained it?" The Traveler put his right hand over the shoulder of the Caelestis. A sympathetic gesture as he was sure that the answer he would receive would bring great pain to Tsadqiel.

"Not quite. Everything was straightforward before the raid of the Fates. We knew our roles and played them felicitously, and the

Gardener was by far the most devoted of us. He was attentive and somehow had an answer for just about everything. The Gardener never lifted a sword and yet knew more about warfare tactics than the most elite of us. He had abilities that, until this day, perplexed me and scared most. On the day of the raid, the Gardener was shot in the back and was left unconscious. We found him in a clutter of rubble, kneeling before what he had built. Imagine a creature so verbally gifted, silenced by what he had witnessed that day.

"As you know by now, Daystar overlooked the search for the item she helped steal in the first place, and many creatures died in a needless campaign. From that day onward, The Gardener never smiled, didn't rebuild, didn't say a thing. He became another broken thing in The Garden until the day he vanished.

"Anon, after his disappearance, I deviated from a search party as he called out to me. Of all the Caelestis he could have called upon, why he chose me still eludes me. But I listened. He told me that he was in a world of wonder that used anima as a means to produce things beyond belief, but instead of anima, they call it mana. I hurried as fast as my wings could carry me and headed toward the third planet of an uncharted star system.

"The far-flung planet was still beyond my reach, but my brother continued calling out to me. He told me that, of all creatures on that backwater planet, a child possessed the book. The child claimed that every living thing that came in contact with the hollowed tome became ill or suffered a sudden horrific death. The neophyte magician told the Gardener that his master died while believing that the sacred item was the solution for vanquishing the evil that plagued his world, but the child disagreed. The child said the book was cursed, as many of his friends, including his master, died protecting it. As he was the only one who could hold it, the young boy figured that he was cursed as well. The young apprentice became disheartened and was ready to relinquish the book to my brother under two conditions.

"First, the boy needed assurance that no harm would come to my brother. The Gardener had to come close to it, close enough to the book to graze it lightly in passing. I forewarned him of the consequences, but my brother did not heed my counsel. The Gardener pressed his index finger through the engravings, and the book was enveloped in soft light, calling out to him by his real name. Assured that my brother passed the first test, the young apprentice asked for something unexpected.

"He wanted to know what the book said, as the writing within it was indecipherable. I yelled in defiance until my voice hoarsened, but it was too late," says a broken-hearted Tsadqiel.

"What happened?" a fervid Traveler asks.

"What do you think happened, idiot? He read it, of course!" answers Daystar as she slowly approaches the Traveler and Tsadqiel.

"He is no fool, Daystar. The only fool amongst us is me. The Gardener didn't reach out to me at all that day, did he?" Tsadqiel wears a smirk when he asks Daystar a question to which he already suspected the answer.

"A few talks of warfare strategies do not constitute a bond of trustworthiness, of friendship. Tell me then, brother, why would he reach out to you at all?" Daystar asks in a deriding way.

"He wouldn't. He called the single Caelestis he trusted most. You manage to interlink our thoughts. That's why there were miscommunications in our conversations. I attributed his prattle to the trauma he suffered, but he wasn't talking to me at all." Tsadqiel surmises as a dumbstruck Traveler listens in.

"You should give yourself more credit, brother. You are not as stupid as you think," says Daystar as she claps in a celebratory way.

"You made sure I listened in, knowing perfectly well that I was righteous, that I will not hesitate to judge him if need be. But your well-crafted plan hit a snag in the end, didn't it?" Tsadqiel asks with a scoff.

"That is why a great general creates countermeasures, and a grunt such as yourself is left twiddling his thumbs," Daystar retorts, stooping down and looking at Tsadqiel with intimidating intent.

"That was your scheme all along. Wasn't it? You beguiled and exploited the desperate need of an exile's wish to be accepted, to finally establish a meaningful connection with one of his own. You somehow convinced him that it was for the good of your people to take the book away from this place." The Traveler intrudes, breaking up Daystar and Tsadqiel's heated discussion.

"The spineless wretch speaks! I thought I beat that ability out of you." Daystar shifts her attention to the Traveler while conveying a disturbing grin.

"Not for lack of trying. But I am glad to be yet another proven example of your many failures," says the Traveler, trying his best to hide a smile.

"Where you see failure, I see opportunities for betterment in the art of imparting divine wrath. You have contracted sophomaniac tendencies from my brother, Traveler. Let me knock you both off of your respective soapboxes. He didn't hand out the sacred tome to me willingly. I didn't expect him to. Besides any feelings he had developed for me, I knew his loyalty to the old man, our Lord, was unwavering. You should have seen the heartbroken look on his face when I asked for the book. It is the same sorrowful stare that a pup gives his owner when he knows he is about to get beaten and have his nose shoved in his excrement," says a relishing Daystar while her brother and the Traveler look at her with disdain.

"I honestly thought that you had made a change for the better. You had us all fooled," Tsadqiel says somberly.

"As the humanoids say, brother, some people make a one-hundred-and-eighty-degree turn; I just took it a bit further and came full circle. Speaking of turns, that's what he did after he saw I wasn't leaving without it. He turned his back on me and stood between the sacred tome and myself. He got what was coming to him. That blast ran through his pathetic body like a blade." Daystar put on a play involving mimicry and pantomiming the pain of the Gardener.

"He didn't call out to you at all. You reached out to him, didn't you? You begged and pleaded for forgiveness. You put on another show, and he forgave you." The Traveler did his best to try to decipher Daystar's methods of madness.

"It was more straightforward than you shall ever know, Traveler. I reached out, and he wagged his tail. He craved normalcy, to go back to how things were. For him, retrieving the book was the only way." Daystar looks upward as her army amasses, nearing the gates of the Kingdom.

"And that was your fallacy, Daystar. You wanted to know the sacred tome's enigmas but not be held accountable for the sin that came with it. You planned to trick the Gardener into reading it for you. The precept is clear about the fate of those who read it. However, it does not mention anything regarding hearing about it. You purposely left me out of that part of the conversation. I thought you were trying to persuade him to stop, but you were screaming in his head only one thing." Tsadqiel looks at Daystar with contempt.

"Read it and tell me! Over and over again. But he never did. Instead, he only said one thing to me; 'it's all a lie.' And then he screamed, across the stars and throughout the heavens, one word, 'LIES!' The rest, of course, you know, as you were there when the old man ordered us to throw him into the Void, alongside with that accursed book. That's how our father deals with these sorts of things, smite it or throw it beneath the giant interstellar rug, which is where you will eventually wind up, too, Traveler. Well, I have an engagement I must attend. It boosts morale when their newly appointed leader is among their ranks in war. Tsadqiel, I will see you on the battlefield either on my side or the wrong one." Daystar flaps her wings and stands mid-air, contemplating her brother. That's when Traveler sees an opportunity to spit in her face one last time.

"His name!" The Traveler shouts, looking directly at Daystar's eyes. "You cannot bring yourself to say it, can you? The Gardener's name? Say it!" he says defiantly.

"Logos. His name was Logos. The old man wants a word with you, Traveler. Make it quick so I can end two plagues with one strike of my sword." Daystar flies away at lightning speed, leaving her brother and an anxious Traveler behind.

Do you know fear?

Mallory?

Fear is a dark abyss and a dreadful shadow prowling within, with glowing eyes that follow your every move.

What happened to the Traveler, Mallory?

It gives out a taste of acidic retch. Fear smells like putrid flesh; it looks like a bloated, maggot-infected beast that awakens at just the right time. It feels like drowning in a sea of sharded glass.

Envoy! Focus on your task at hand!

That sound. That terrible sound your unbridled heartbeat creates that makes you envy the dead.

Enough! Your childish frights are a waste of my time! Focus your attention on the Traveler, or I swear your fate will be worse than any nightmare imaginable.

He looks up and sees a lurid sky filled with winged creatures that carry murderous weapons of war. He is concerned but no longer afraid. They talk.

The Traveler and his newfound friend. The one who killed his brother, the one who saved him from a fatal fate. They talk about someone who should not be mentioned—the Gardener.

A gardener? I think the few electrical synapses left in you are turning into ectoplasm goop, like the rest of your body.

No, he is the key—the unremembered among them. He is like them but different. Each birth and name of their kin they remember, but not his. Always at the tip of their tongue, an elusive name and origin make him untrustworthy. He was a sculptor of amazing things, passionate, humble, and kind to all, his Lord's favorite. Until a deeply wounded betrayal stole his reason to be. They took the sacred book and left him broken along with all his creations.

And across the cosmos, you will not find a more accurate account of how the Universe came to be than the written words in that book. I know of this tale already. Move on.

How could you? It is forbidden to read it!

Mallory, focus! The Traveler?

She tricked him! He read it! Not aloud, but to himself.

Mallory, enough!

No! You can't outrun that kind of pain, hatred, and so much rage. The one he loved above all failed him! He disposed of him like garbage—his favorite son!

I SAID ENOUGH! He is no son of his! He never was! Tell me about the Traveler, or I will erase you from existence.

She approaches.

Who?

Daystar. Her Lord wants to see the Traveler. She is going to war, turning brother against brother. On this day, many shall fall.

Interesting.

Your son. How could you?

...

FINAL JUDGMENT

DEAFENING WAILS AND SCREAMS pierce the heavens above. The cosmos and its stars were no longer visible, as a crimson dye stained the firmaments. Now the red turns to a pale gray as the ember remains of dead Caelestis fall like snow. A storm of falling ash fills the antechamber. Tsadqiel extends his left arm with his palm upward to catch a falling flake of what remained of his fallen kin.

"Are you not going to fight?" the terrified Traveler asks Tsadqiel.

"In another time, I would have been there, battling abreast with my brothers and sisters, defending righteousness and the will of my Lord. After the events that transpired, I feel that it is not my place to do so anymore," Tsadqiel retorts while clenching his left hand into a fist, further breaking apart the fallen flake. The wetness of his palm deliquesces the ashen particle into coagulated blood.

"What would you do then?" the concerned Traveler asks.

"You have received the highest honor, to look upon the face of my Lord. A blessing I shall never experience, even if I get to live for another millennium. I will do what was in my nature to do before I turned into this instrument of judgment and destruction. I will guard your way into the sacred halls, but no further, I'm afraid. But this I pledge to you, while I still draw breath, I will remain here waiting for your arrival," Tsadqiel says to the Traveler with a smile.

The drained Traveler staggers to rise but does so by leaning against the shoulder of the Caelestis. Tsadqiel dislodges his sword from the floor. With a simple orison, the sharp instrument of death morphs into an elegant walking stick for the Traveler to lean on. The Traveler begins his slow wayfaring through the antechamber and into the entrance of the sacred halls. He turns back to look at the unlikely ally he made in Tsadqiel.

"What if I don't make it out? Would you wait here forever?" the Traveler asks in jest.

"Peace be with you, Traveler. May you find the answers to the questions that burden you." Tsadqiel offers a respectful bow.

The stir of echoing screams quells gradually as the Traveler limps into the sacred halls. The engraving of the walls has been, for the most part, preserved. Providentially, the wave of destruction that claimed the other architectural wonders of this place curtailed three feet from the entrance. The Traveler hobbles through the dimly lit corridor with the aid of his walking stick. Battered and bruised, the enfeebling creature fails to overlook the magnificent wall etchings. If Daystar had not damaged his peripheral vision, he would have found the prominent carving at his left familiar. For now, the Traveler focuses on reaching the doorway that leads to the adjacent room.

Nearing the threshold, before the Traveler has an opportunity to touch it, a harmony of mechanical whirls, accompanied by shooting steam, causes the doors to open. After the thin curtain of dust clears, the Traveler enters a foyer filled with statues and carvings similar to those left behind in the antechamber beside The Garden. However, the quality of the engravings is subpar in comparison. It doesn't take a connoisseur to know that the author of these sculptures is someone other than the Gardener.

Three gigantic ritual aediculae built into the walls deceive the Traveler as he takes his third step into the antechamber. Within each niche space, three colossal statues stand out from the rest of the carvings. The triumvirate sculptures sit clockwise from each other on separate thrones. The menacing figures had either been defaced or beheaded by a set of raging blows, making them unidentifiable. Although this is the first time the Traveler has encountered the three giant statues, their characteristics are conspicuously familiar.

Counterclockwise, the first statue appears to be of a woman extending her arms charitably. The head portion of the figure seems to have been ripped asunder by sheer strength. The next statue is a humanoid extending his right arm, pointing his finger judgingly. A jeweled crown sits atop his brow. The figure had also fallen victim to vandalization. Savagely carved out by an act of vengeance, the face of the judging male is unrecognizable. Lastly, another beheaded statue sits on his luxurious throne. The male figure has his arm extended forth; however, it seems someone has torn off the limb midway. A detached fist lies before the feet of the colossus. It appears as if he is clenching a strange device of unknown origin.

A smoothed-out blind wall, bearing only one symbol, lies next to the statues. The wall dimensions are similar to the space taken by one of the three figures. The wall seems to be a late addition to the rest of the architecture. Taken aback by the etched markings on the wall, the Traveler thinks back to his first encounter with the Caelestis, and I, the Ghost in the shadows.

"Come closer, Law-Lord. Long have I waited for your arrival."

A booming voice emanates from the hallway next to the blind wall. The echoing call reverberates, making the structure quake, but the words are only audible by those attuned to divinity.

The tremor causes The Traveler to fall to the unforgiving floor. His walking stick rolls away five feet; under his current condition, it might as well be five miles. He begins the strenuous task of crawling slowly through the hallway to get to the call source. The closer he gets to his journey's end, the weaker he becomes.

Halfway into the hall, his limbs tremble from lack of strength until they give out. His face once again is marred by the sudden impact with the ground. With the bit of power he has left, he drags himself until he reaches the next doorway. Fatigued, the Traveler rolls on his back and sees the statues of two Caelestis supporting the arch of the entryway. The one on the right is unrecognizable to him. However, the one at his left, he knows all too well. Perhaps this is an omen of an upcoming calamity for him. The visage of Daystar featured on a prominent entrance is never a good sign. At a journey's end, the weary Traveler grows listless from the pain and closes his eyes, surrendering to whatever outcome.

"Law-Lord! The truth-seeker of officious demeanor, raging with fury, carrying out the heaviest of burdens, with lips full of resentment and a tongue that lashes out with consuming fire, now lies at my doorstep, overwhelmed by despair! You have come this close but no further! Low you have fallen! You have turned into a defeatist!"

The overwhelming, thunderous words rattle the Traveler's brain.

"Mercy. I've endured insufferable pain. Through your guardians, I've known your wrath. I came seeking answers; now, I only ask for leniency," the dying Traveler pleads as a blinding light forces him to shut his eyes.

As the light dims, the Traveler finds himself elsewhere. He sees glowing plinths at the base of enormous, emblazoned pillars that seem to go on forever. Attached to them are memorials and handcrafted images of Caelestis, affording a downward view of this colossal room's stone floor. Quartz stones run in circles around the room, forming pathways leading to the main entrance, a door at the rear left of the chamber, and a four-sided throne in the middle of the room. The seats adorned with embellished corners, meant for the quadrumvirate occupants, remain, for the most part, empty. The Traveler finds himself standing behind a mirrored, polished lectern that faces one side of the four-sided throne chairs.

Gazing at his reflection, he sees an elderly Black gentleman. He is balding, with a semicircle of grey hair that meets at his sides. His face is faded, timeworn, bearing grey, frizzy, spade-shaped facial hair. His eyes are aged and blood-flecked. He is wearing a jacket with a vest underneath and a pair of trousers made of fine linen, complimenting his contour, broadening his upper torso, and narrowing his waist. The common purpose of an ensemble of this sort is to provide a regal look. An invisible line forms from the chest to his shoes to enhance his presence. But the only thing holding up the posture of the slightly hunched Traveler is the cane bequeathed to him.

"What is this? What has become of me? If this is your mercy, I do not want it! All I've sought were the answers to questions that plague my very existence! All I've found is a truth by consensus that claims that as far as the universe pertains, my life has no intrinsic value! That I am nothing more than a disease! For that, I've been bludgeoned and humiliated! On the verge of death, I have come to the source of all things! To seek enlightenment, not to be remade into a species I detest!" The Traveler ponders a plethora of other existential questions while looking at his withered and veiny hands.

The grinding sound of stones breaks the silence as the four-sided throne begins to turn slowly.

"You disapprove of this vessel? It is like your kin to be lovers of self, boastful, and proud! Your race is disobedient and ungrateful! How very shortsighted of you to bear the same flaws. Filial piety is deeply rooted in most civilizations in the Universe, for there is undoubtedly nothing more prized by a creature than its wisdom. Though life takes away everything else, knowledge is the one thing that remains."

The words and the grinding sound of stones echo throughout the otherworldly structure.

"It is knowledge I seek, nothing more! I came before you to know the truth! Not to be turned into this bag of bones! After all this time, I have served my elders as a Law-Lord to maintain order and eradicate chaos! Rightness versus injustice! Now my elders tell me there's no discernible line between the two! That we have committed an unforgivable transgression against you, our maker! I stand before you an unwavering herald of order, and my just reward for a lifetime of obedience is becoming an object of further ridicule!" The Traveler pounds the top of the podium with all the strength that an eighty-five-year-old man can muster. With tears rolling from his eyes, he does not know what to believe anymore.

"ENOUGH!"

The Traveler's tantrum ends with a very familiar earsplitting scold. The echoing sound intensifies as a shadowy creature sitting in one of the throne chairs approaches. The curvilinear trajectory of the throne chair comes to an abrupt end. The face of a familiar figure leans forward, away from the shadows. Abruptly, the Traveler is thrust backward through time and space, eons when the Known Universe is still young, and thus he is witness to his species' birth from a particular point of view.

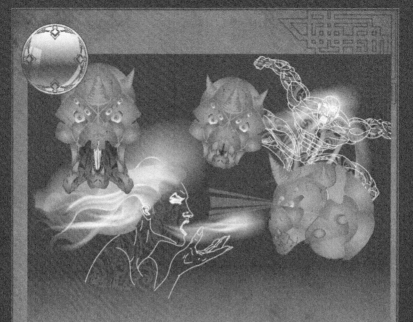

An excerpt from The Book of the Universal Bylaw
THE FATES

I AM THE LIGHT, and my shadow is darkness; I make harmony and create calamity; I am your Lord, who does all these things. It was so that I culled you each from this very light and the dark. I gave you the boon of Universal Law to maintain balance among all creations within the Universe.

But you overstepped your prescribed roles, becoming masters of the duality of light and darkness, and did so by taking decisive roles— haughty children, forgetful of who breathed life onto you! Do you think your power is higher than the one who abides within you?

You forsook your purpose and became morally defined as benevolent and malevolent entities catering to the mythos created by those beneath you. You ignited a nugatory war to prove which one is above the other, lest you forget that I am the one above all!

You became The Fates of Order and Chaos and deceived the superstitious and the gullible to assert yourselves as the Universe's only authority. In your arrogant game of chance, you committed unpardonable sins! You affronted your creator with preternatural creations—demigods, monsters, titans, immortals, abominations to fight on your respected sides!

Your unnatural horrors had run rampant, far too long unchecked! You have condemned yourselves and everything from above and below with a Nocuous Plague! A virulent disease carried out by the upbringing of creatures that should not be! Your creations infected The Known Universe, creating carcinogenic paradoxes!

Vehemently I called upon your breed to rebuke them for their transgressions, but they undermined their creator, plotting against me! I say onto you; I cursed the day I breathed life into your kindred! For the iniquity of your forebearers, I look upon you with cynical eyes and avenging desire! I am vengeful and wrathful; you will know my fury when I unleash my vengeance upon you!

Jolted back to reality, The Traveler finds himself behind the lustrous podium facing the Lord of the Kingdom and sovereign of the heavens. A sense of paramnesia sets in as he contemplates the face of his creator. A false memory, a glitch of this vessel, or was it something that I said that stuck with him? The fading, echoing words resound throughout the throneroom and reverberate stronger over the frail human body of the Traveler.

Any other creature in existence would have a mental collapse after being shown the origin of their species. Moreover, they would have thoughts of worthlessness, an immense and swelling sense of guilt accompanied by a detachment from self, from reality. Their hearts would burst from their chest after the so-called creator of all things accused them of universal genocide.

Surprisingly, the Traveler remains calm. He has seen this type of deception before. From his elders, from the mystic creatures, he surveys— sleight of hands and pretty lights that even he at one time has employed.

Through his creator's narrative, the Traveler discovers how a skewed perspective fed into digestible factoids can twist a particular set of events, through omissions and misleading accounts, with the intended goal of retconning historical facts that will benefit the interest of one individual. It is not unprecedented for a deity to tell a tale filled with the foible traits of mortals. But this is the creator of all things. Why would he lie?

"Forgive me, my Lord. I thought we acted at your behest. The Council of Order—" the soft-spoken Traveler is interrupted by an outburst of rage from his maker.

"It is a farce! They are masters of pious claptraps that beguile fools like you to commit deplorable wickedness on their behalf! You are the supreme example of the wrongdoings of your so-called council! A bastardly byproduct of an unholy union! Your guilt is unforgivable, for it is by birthright!"

The miscarriage of divine justice against him is over before it begins. The Traveler finds himself on the verge of judgment. All that crosses his mind is that the judge's physiognomy is somewhat familiar to whom I referred to as Helō'hēm; however, some key elements were absent. His interstellar enamel seems to have faded, losing its luster. His jeweled crown was missing alongside the rest of the Natural Order of Things members. The conjoined quartet of metagalactic justice was just one. Did I lie when I spoke to him about how the Universe or its wonders came to be?

"At a time, it seemed clear. Chaos against Order, evil versus virtue, this was my only indoctrination. I acted according to my doctrine as if it were a divine mandate. I thought I was on the side of righteousness, and I shepherd the destiny of mortals by ruling over their fate. Unbeknownst to me, this was not our intended purpose," the Traveler explains.

Even though the Traveler sounds numb and hollowed out by his maker's encounter, his apologetic retort is not without merit. He is just a simple cog in a machine that has set catastrophic events in motion. Chastised and condemned by following the simplest of orders, to become a herdsman of the creatures beneath and lead them to righteousness. But he is not without guilt. Over time, his victories over Chaos have made him prideful. More than once, he has resorted to skulduggery tactics to win by any means necessary.

"Vacuous creature! What the ignoramus with the strictest of prejudice rules is pride, the unfailing wrongdoings of fools! A perversion among your kin that has gone unchecked far too long! It was never about the triumph of one against the other!"

"Balance. It was not the toppling of one over the other. My kind was supposed to maintain balance."

"Law-Lord, you poor deluded creature; it is only at the end that you understand. Say not that I am without mercy and graciousness, for I am slow to wrath and bountiful in love and fidelity. I can forgive iniquity, transgressions, and sin. But by all means, you shall not be granted a complete absolution! The stain of the sinful behavior of your lineage runs deep within you. It is onto you, the last of your kind, that I, the creator of all things, burden upon you the misdeeds of your ancestry! I sentence you, the last of your kind, to walk and live among those you detest! Not as an agent of Order or Chaos but as the only living amalgamation of the two. You shall be known as the living conundrum, a creature who employs the gift of what comes naturally to bring Order and resorts to your counterparts' most heinous misdeeds to inflict Chaos. You will not rule over them. You shall walk among them, ignored, without receiving reverence or praise. As you said earlier, you shall provide balance."

"How will I do this?"

"On the third planet of a remote region, you will find Vergil, keeper of Destiny. I have outlined to the simpleminded what would seem like a convoluted plan. She will guide you in your mission."

"What mission?"

"In times of great calamities, from among the Earth's wicked, you shall cull the chosen to ascend to Luminaries. They shall redirect the course of humankind's destiny from mutually assured destruction to prosperity. On the day no other Luminaries are found, you will know that I will unleash my final judgment upon all, including yourself!"

An incredible rumble shakes the abode of the Traveler's creator. Once again, the Traveler falls to the floor. While the place seems to crumble, a glowing trinket bounces on the floor toward his direction. It is the emblem Daystar scratched against the void. If the key were to unlock the cell, it would undoubtedly undo all of creation. The Traveler catches it midair and quickly hides it in his garments while his creator looks around him in distress.

"Something terrible has transpired."

The anxious creator murmurs to himself as his abode continues to shake.

"My Lord, Daystar, has betrayed you. There is an interstellar war occurring at this moment."

"That war began and ended as it was ordained to be! Daystar assumed her new role as I asked of her. This happening is something else. Something unplanned, unforeseen. Go and unburden me no more Law-Lord! Fulfill your purpose!"

The Traveler stands with his cane's help and begins hobbling toward the exit of the creator's chamber; he finds himself once more revitalized with some of the power he once possessed flowing through him. But before the Traveler can make it past the door, a stern warning comes from his creator.

"The talisman you have hidden in your pocket is not a plaything, Law-Lord! You are sorely mistaken if you think it is a weapon you can wield against me!"

The Traveler halts and freezes midway, exiting the arch of the entryway.

"By hoarding it, you have inadvertently chosen to become its keeper—a burden that will eat at your very core! That medallion is one of the most powerful artifacts in all creation. However, this is a power not meant to be utilized or exploited! It will not grant you abilities beyond what you are capable of already! It will test your fortitude to the brink of total corruption! With time, it will become unbearably tiresome to carry. But like the stain of mortal sin, it will never leave your side. The nature of the dark force that inhabits the talisman is to destroy the wearer's morality and reason. You will not wield it; it will wield you! The medallion has a will of its own, and like many things in creation, it wants to achieve its purpose. It's a key desperately wanting to reach the door it was made to open. When the time comes to reunite both door and talisman, you will set about the end of everything."

The Traveler reaches into his pocket, grabbing hold of the talisman with the intent of tossing it toward the shadows from which it came. But he finds it is beyond his will to do so. He most likely will gouge his own eyes out before parting with it.

"Your actions denote the mistrustfulness of my words! Even in the presence of your maker, you still behave like a heathen! Let me assure you, Law-Lord, that like the unredeemable stain of mortal sin, the talisman will not leave you! Not until I declare it so! Leave my sight and burden me with your presence no more!"

The Traveler limps out of the sacred halls and into the antechamber. Once again, he finds himself immersed in his thoughts. His elders, The Ghost in the shadows, the Caelestis, and his maker, the creator of everything, in one way, all lied.

He walks onward into The Garden toward the only creature that has always been truthful by his estimation. After all, Tsadqiel promised to be there upon his return.

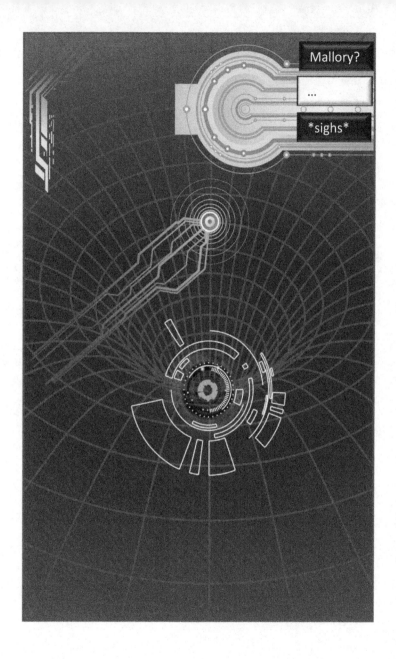

Mallory?

...

sighs

ENEMY MINE

THE SOLEMN ECHO OF THE cane striking the floor breaks the overpowering silence that stays with the Traveler until he reaches the entrance of the antechamber. Falling particles of an unknown origin obscure his field of vision as he takes his first steps into what was once the most beautiful place in the universe. The Traveler tries to make out a luminous aureate silhouette sitting afar on the fallen column where he once shared a moment of peace with his newfound friend. Something else can be felt in the air, the unnatural tranquility that belongs to a burial ground. A sensation he felt upon his arrival now seems to have spread like a gangrenous disease throughout the entire Kingdom. Abruptly, an oppressive and overwhelming force of malice makes its presence felt, suffocating the tranquility of nothingness.

Out of the mist, a grimalkin-type beast pounces in the Traveler's direction. The four-digit claws, including an innermost hidden dewclaw, penetrate her chosen victim's chest, knocking him down in the process. Hisses and growls accompany a barrage of swift attacks toward the face of her game. Instinctively, the Traveler tries his best to protect the vessel he not so long ago cursed from the sinister beast attempting to claw out his eyes. It only takes a quick swing of his cane to cause the furry creature to jump from his torso to the adjacent floor.

Looking upon the physiognomy of his aggressor, the Traveler finds himself bewildered by its appearance. The unholy concoction is composed primarily of what seems to be a small domestic feline and pieces of hellish creatures. The sinister animal circles her prey, trilling and hissing as she waits for the Traveler to incorporate himself into a kneeling position.

"Even in this infernal form, I succeed in making you bow before me!" the feline creature says amidst yowling while sitting before the Traveler.

A shiny golden tag that swings from the beast's collar stands out from her chest. An engraving on the golden tag bears the same language that adorns The Garden walls. Before the beast can attempt to claw out her enemy's eyes for a second time, a voice command halts her attack.

> "Daystar! Scat!" the beast, of mauve and white fur, withdraws slowly, receding into the distance, lost in the mist, until her eerie eyes are no longer visible.

A helping hand enveloped in radiant light extends out of the mist and reaches toward the distressed Traveler.

> "Don't you find it extraordinary how a noteworthy occasion such as this can bring together folks who are otherwise stark in contrast from each other?"

There is something in the stranger's method of words that brings warmth and peace to the Traveler's heart as he converses with a beguiling pitch using soothing tones that could easily be mistaken for a dear friend's voice.

Still distraught by his encounter with the beast, the Traveler senses a strange comfort as this outlander draws closer to him. The Traveler feels relief from the pain and constraints he has carried since his encounter with the Caelestis. All feelings of grief and distress seem to dissipate for the moment.

As the radiated being draws closer, the incandescence surrounding him diminishes enough for the Traveler to notice the strange attire that covers most of his skin. The outlander wears flowing robes of a blood-red shade, a tabard, an undertunic, and a hooded cloak with golden ribbons sewn in an intricate pattern attached to the edges. A pair of gauntlets with a similar intrinsic design and knee-high boots of the same color complete his attire. Past the stranger's gimcrack ensemble, an electroluminescent azure mane extends far from its reaches beyond the protection of the hood. His skin seems soft, of a creamy alabaster tone. His eyes, however, are another spectacle altogether.

While his irises' peculiar shade of turquoise expresses trustworthiness, and the glow of blue and green from his corneas emanates the calming love of friendship, his pupils tell another story. Within those dots of absolute black, swirling abysses filled with the purest of evil lingers, waiting to devour the ensnared soul.

Snapping out of the spellbinding trance induced by the presence of the outlander, the Traveler rejects the helping hand scornfully and carefully leans on the cane as his aches and pains quickly return. The Traveler straightens up as upright as his backaches allow him. He stares upward as the stranger surpasses him by three inches.

"Who are you?" asks the visibly upset Traveler.

"As rude as it is to answer a question with another, I feel it is only fair to answer your query first, as my eagerness to meet another living soul in this desolated place has infringed on my manners as of late," the outlander replies calmly as the Traveler seems noticeably confused.

"I apologize," says the Traveler as his head begins to throb, resulting from the bewildering effects of the outlander's presence.

"Don't be. I was rude to you beforehand, as introductions are of the utmost importance. Trustworthiness and transparency are crucial to all conversations. By my estimation, that is the virtue of introducing oneself. You need to engage the hearer into listening attentively to avoid future unpleasantries." The Traveler's patience wears thin as the outlander explains himself using all sorts of graceful gesticulations.

"Where is Tsadqiel? What happened to this place?" The Traveler stares upward, directly into the eyes of the outlander.

"But dear friend, you haven't allowed me the time to answer your first query yet. It is worthy of high praise to have an inquisitive mind. Still, your lack of prudence edges on impertinence." The smug outlander crosses his arms and wags his finger at the Traveler while elevating a meter above the floor. His garments and cape flutter slowly and lightly as if they sway with the wind, but there is no breeze felt within The Kingdom.

"Friends, I have but one, and you are certainly not him! I've grown tired of your evasiveness! For the last time, who or what are you?" The Traveler angrily points his cane toward the outlander as a warning.

The outlander raises further in the air and poises himself with his arms wide open as his garments ripple violently like a tarpaulin caught amid a maelstrom. The white sclera of his eyes turns to blood, and a malignant smirk etches across his face. His body radiates unbridled power in the form of blinding azure light. Without warning, a tempest of energy emerges from him, haphazardly bombarding the floor below. The energy current pierces and splits the ground apart, and each beam converges underneath, turning into a blast wave of cataclysmic proportions that overruns the entirety of The Kingdom.

Meter-sized radiation blisters surface all over the antechamber floor and far beyond it. They spread quickly like an unholy disease transforming the formerly empyrean surface into a cluster of bursting points. Each blister erupts, spewing a destructive force that begins tearing the megaregion asunder. The booming voice of the outlander overlaps the dissonance of chaos among the cluttering noise.

"I was the stone that the builder discarded! Now I've become the foundation of his downfall! Let him tremble and despair!"

Betwixt the whirlwind of wreckage and the booming explosions, the Traveler struggles vigorously to cling to a piece of the floor that begins to disintegrate exceedingly.

With quivering lips, he shrieks a plead, "You'll kill us all! Please stop!"

In less than no time, the Traveler finds himself seated, without a hair out of place, on the same fallen column where his friend said he would wait for him. Beside him sits the outlander, juggling three unusual spheres of vile and virulent malice. Two alternating electrical charges keep the glassy orbs together. Around and around, they move gracefully, barely touching the tip of his fingers. The Traveler grasps his shirt, trying to catch his breath and ease his chest pain, staring blankly at the iridescent-colored spheres.

"It felt real!" says the Traveler between short gasps of breath as the intense tightening of his chest halts.

"Why would you think otherwise?" asks the outlander as he puffs the carcinogenic element away from his hands and into the heavens.

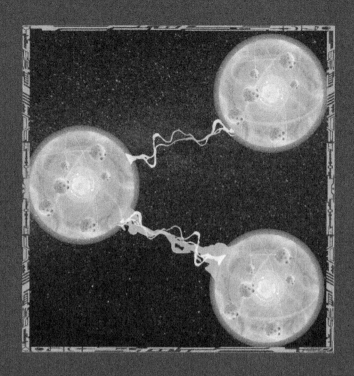

"I've witnessed countless deities, mystics, and charlatans pull illusions of a similar magnitude. In all my years as a Law-Lord, it never made me flinch, not once, let alone bring me to the point of death. It might be yet another unforeseen side-effect of this meat suit! I have succumbed to the hallucinations of a crazed mud chimp!" says the Traveler, running his hands over his eyes.

"It's not the meat suit you wear that impedes your sanity; your perspective is skewed. Never again confuse me with a magician of cheap illusions. I can warp reality beyond those possessing nigh omnipotence. I destroyed this place with the same ease a child levels a miniature sandcastle and restored you and everything around you with a simple thought just because you asked politely," the outlander says with a smile.

A true theophany has just introduced himself to a heathen that used to oversee the livelihood of gods. It will seem that destiny has a wicked sense of humor as the transpired event ruthlessly defies the Traveler's ethos.

A visually shaken Traveler looks with widening eyes toward the antechamber entrance, and his thoughts travel past its walls and into the throne room, where he previously met his creator. Intuitively he tries to reach out to his keeper, the one who branded him with the totality of the sin of his brethren, who inflicted sorrow, torture, and humiliation on him, an unbeknownst sinner. The Traveler reaches out to his maker, the same one that cursed his existence and offered salvation through a path of meagerness and shame because no one is above redemption, and his love is infinite.

"Don't bother calling out to him. The old-timer left while you made your slow, triumphal entrance," says the outlander as he opens his cloak and takes out an item that, although the Traveler sees for the first time, looked very familiar.

The gleaming artifact of radiant gold appears like a book, but the fore-edge text block opposing the spine seems to be sealed shut. A long chain ties the outlander's left gauntlet to one of the book's raised bands. Of all the wonders, the lustrous artifact possesses only one that shocked the Traveler to his very core. An inscription on the book cover is identical to the one engraved on Daystar's amulet. The Traveler reaches within the pocket that holds the accursed item. The proximity of both relics causes the Traveler to envision memories that are not his own. Remembrances of a time long ago when Daystar beguiled the creature sitting beside him into reading from the exact text he now holds.

"Logos! You are Logos, the Gardener!" The Traveler clenches his shirt pocket.

"Do you know the meaning of that name?" The outlander polishes the gilded book in his hands with his crimson cloak.

"I can't say that I do."

"In our native tongue, Logos refers to the spoken word of the Lord, as it communicates his ability to set things in motion or express his resolve. He speaks, and through me, he creates. Logos was my slave name. After my forced exile, I have chosen a new name for myself. You may call me Malefactor, patron saint of ungodly deeds." Malefactor turns to the Traveler with a sinister stare and a vile smirk.

"I am called the Traveler by many."

"What a mundane moniker they have chosen for you," says a chuckling Malefactor.

"That is not my given name. It is simply something that the Voice in the Void called me. My name is Alister, former Law-Lord for the Council of Order. Wait, why would I tell you any of this? You are using your influence on me again, aren't you?" Just as the Traveler begins to restore some of his composure, his arrhythmia returns.

"Don't belittle yourself; it cannot be helped. It's the same as breathing is to a mud-monkey. It comes effortlessly. You should see the things creatures of sovereignty confess to me in a most disreputable manner. It is both sad and hilarious. I must say that your resiliency to my influence is extraordinary. Only those gifted with omniscience can fend it off," Malefactor says as he gives a congratulatory slap to the Traveler's shoulder.

"So, you talk to the Voice in the Void? How is the old hag?" Malefactor asks as the Traveler slides away from him and centers his mind.

"Under lock and key, where she can rot for all eternity while she sells her lies and tales to another passerby!" says the Traveler as he peers at Malefactor with disdain.

"To some, we might be supernatural forces of profound immorality and wickedness that do not obey or conform to any standards or principles regarding the distinction between what is universally deemed right and wrong. We may very well lack the qualities of mercy and compassion, and our methodology can be viewed as cruel and barbaric, utterly odious and wicked, without an iota of emotional connection to our actions. But the one thing you can be assured of is that we are not the teller of untruths. We detest lies and those who blur the lines between the two to justify their actions," Malefactor says as he tries to catch his reflection in the polished book.

"You claim to lack a moral compass and have no mercy, yet you spared my life when I begged you to do so. You acted in contradiction to the things that you now profess. You expect me to believe in the hypocrisy of what you just told me?" the Traveler asks firmly, trying to hide his fear of the creature sitting beside him.

"You regret having a second chance at life, or is it a form of self-gratification that comes from the sheer arrogance of trying to find a flaw in what I profess to be true?" Malefactor glares at the Traveler with blazing eyes. The blue luminance gives way to red.

"I meant no disrespect." The Traveler averts his gaze and looks down at a fresh ashen silhouette burned on the floor at the feet of Malefactor.

"I'm sure you did not. Do you know what I have learned over the years, Traveler? I have realized that deities and creatures of vast power, who have been given the boon to create life, share the same flawed behavioral traits of their creations. Of course, the gods claim to be above such pettiness. But their actions tell otherwise.

"You are not a god; however, you once had the supremacy to infringe upon their lives. Imagine the sheer power it takes to spank a deity when it misbehaves. Hehe! Perverse! You did your job as requested without the aftertaste of hubris. It was not after discovering the truth behind your trade that you succumbed to all those unpleasant traits of humanoid behavior.

"You are the conception of a creation that should not have been made in the first place. You have been humiliated and tamed—suffered through demoralization with the intended purpose of reconstruction and repurpose—to cleanse you of any moral ambiguity and bring you to the same state of indifference you once possessed. When you pleaded with me, I sensed fear. But it was not the fear that abides within the habitual sinner that begs for another chance at life and continues perpetually as a repeat offender. It was the dread of someone who begged for a second chance at life because he felt unfulfilled. Even though they thought you were broken, it would seem that their intended cleansing proved to be unsuccessful. I find your fortitude quite fascinating. It was not an act of mercy on my behalf that has kept you breathing. It's just sheer curiosity, honesty, and good manners. Never underestimate them." His menacing eyes dim and shift in the direction where the Traveler looks—beneath his feet is the ashen stain of a creature that is no more.

"That stain beneath your feet is fresh," says the Traveler as he turns away. His elbows are firmly placed on his thighs, his hands clenched with each finger tightly interlaced, and two thumbs knuckles pressed against his forehead. He holds his bowed head, which grows heavy with overwhelming grief.

"Oh, this thing. It is unfortunate. The mess it leaves behind when it dies. Once you kill one, the stain is seared into the floor, and the remaining ash particles float everywhere. Hence the misty atmosphere. I've meant to get a broom and brush off some of it, but Daystar loves to roll around in it. It's like a giant kitty litter to her. How would you know that is fresh?" asks Malefactor as he wipes some residual ash from his boot's sole.

"The ashes on the floor are of a different shade than those beneath your feet. When I was taken by Daystar and dragged into this accursed place, I saw a residue on the entryway—a pale gray, like a murky snowfall. Then before my very eyes, a fratricide occurred, and I saw a creature's head turn into the same ashen substance. The residue was of a darker shade than the one I previously saw. It was the result of a fresh kill. All the shapes seared on the floor share indistinguishable similarities, but the one beneath your feet belongs to the one who passed judgment on you. You saved him for last and most likely forced him to watch as you destroyed his kind. Beneath your feet are the remains of my friend Tsadqiel!" The Traveler digs his fingernails deep into his skin, making his hands shake.

There is an upsurge of lingering, suppressed anger within the Traveler that has been growing since his capture. It was a spark in the dark that slowly evolved into an inferno. He is a proud creature that had been compelled to bend to the new direction his creator had imposed onto him and did so with acquiescence. He had faith that his only friend in this universe, who also was without purpose, would follow him on his new journey. His credence is now but a stain on the floor, courtesy of his newfound enemy. His antagonist places the infamous golden book on his lap, and through a series of chosen words, Malefactor rubs salt on the Traveler's wound amid congratulatory applauses.

"Look at you, figuring out the answers to your own questions! You are quite the enigma! Solving the complexities that this universe can bring about just by using the tiniest of resources, and by that, I mean the total sum of intellect in your head. I have to say that it is quite an achievement. I think even Daystar would admit that this is quite a feat! Where is that troublemaker?" As the loquacious Malefactor searches for his captive pet, an amber light engulfs the Traveler's body, which painfully burns away his humanoid husk, revealing his original form.

The release of his pent-up hatred is instantaneous. There are no pretty sigils to display, no elegant words of warning. One scream of wrath forces his mouth wide open until it disjoints. His eyelids elongate to the point of rupture. Gaping holes on his hands of scorched tissue make way for the outpouring of sheer hatred transmogrified into raw power. The outpouring blast wrought of loathing and lifeforce is focused and on point.

There is no time for screams, the protective hood covering Malefactor's head turns quickly into ash, and his face melts away in a churn of alabaster and red wax. His skinless head bursts into a fine red mist, revealing parts of his cervical spine. As the blast of energy continues its destructive path, the coveted golden book falls from the keeper's lifeless hands to the ground, denting the already marred floor. The fainting Traveler shares the same fate as his drained body plummets to the kingdom's stones for the last time. His eyes are smoldering, and his stretched-out tongue lies upon a pile of fallen ash on the ground. With only seconds of life left, the Traveler gasps what would seem to be a chuckle.

One millisecond before the entirety of the lifeforce abandons the Traveler, the falling ash flakes pause their descent in midair and begin to ascend. An unforeseen force lifts his body, which twists and turns, gradually returning to where he was seated before his outburst of rage. The treasured book arises to his keeper's lifeless hands, and the dent in the floor is removed. The Traveler sees the blast of destructive force returning toward him like an upcoming bolide threatening to disintegrate him. The energy blast returns from which it came. The moment where the Traveler's eyelid slits, his jaw is unhinged, and the palm of his hands rupture to give way to the blast of pure hatred is fixed in place. Each piece of skin, nerve, bone, and drop of blood spilled belonging to his enemy's head returns to its rightful place. Like a work of art frozen in time, it illustrates an astonishing visual of reckoning.

But not all is the way it was. The falling ash, the slightly tilted head of Malefactor as the beam of energy hit his face, may have been frozen in time, but the eyes of the Traveler, all his pain receptors, and most of his senses are entirely awakened. The pain of the scorching energy rampaging throughout his body is excruciating. His tunnel vision only allows for a blinding glare of light and blurred peripheral sight.

Amid the silence across the Kingdom, echoing steps can be heard approaching the Traveler, where he sits frozen in a glitch of time. Although blurred, his peripheral vision catches a familiar figure walking toward him.

> "The looming shadow beneath when the prey drinks from the river. The firm footing on the brittle terrain belonging to the unsuspected thrill-seeker at the cliff. The ill-informed fortune-hunter violates the dead in search of riches, ignorant of the sigil warnings of curses to all trespassers. I can paint portraits of an infinity of other instances where a creature's poor judgment inevitably caused it to fumble up. But this instance before me, frozen in perpetuity, surmises the sheer collective of universal stupidity." The blurred creature's voice is distinguishable to the Traveler. The vocal sound is that of an amused Malefactor.

The Traveler's scream, made of shooting pain, frustration, fear, and anger, is muffled by his paralysis. A low pitch groan is the best he can accomplish, an effort that Malefactor rewards with a series of pats on his head.

"When I first laid eyes upon you, I saw a powerful yet conflicted creature. I sensed an intense yearning within you, an unbridled craving often found in those who abuse their faculty for desire. You crave that which you had come to know as normalcy. You lust after the power and freedom you once had as a Law-Lord." The suffering Traveler desperately tries to catch a glimpse of Malefactor's actions as he moves about.

"As I said earlier, you've been repurposed. Your creator gave you a new vocation and role. However, even before his tongue rested on the roof of his mouth, acedia dominated your thoughts as you grew indifferent to your new-found duties and obligations." Malefactor speaks as he walks toward his other self.

"The medallion you carry has been said to be the one thing that holds power to tip the balance in favor or against the Universe's welfare. Like the longing for material possessions that inflicts a humanoid's mind, you saw it shining in the darkness and instantly wanted it. That emblem in your hands is a glittery trinket, yet you hold it with a rapacious desire. You are not cursed, Traveler. It is only your greed that will not let you part with it." Through his blurred vision, the Traveler watches the creature known as Malefactor retrieve the golden book from the lap of his doppelganger.

"If you could only see yourself, see what you have become—a misanthrope of hatred consumed by the uncontrolled feelings of anger and rage. The news of your departed friend was the drop that caused the spill of the unmitigated wrath within you. Your wish for vengeance overwhelmed you to the point of this self-destructive behavior," says Malefactor as he moves out of the traveler's field of vision.

"I find it odd that the news of Tsadqiel's passing affected you so much. Considering your state of mind upon hearing of a higher authority superseding yours, it is well in your nature the covetousness of such power to remain at the top of the food chain. His kindness was a bonding experience during your martyrdom, but how long would that allegiance have lasted when you'd finally find each other at odds? Your new role will make you a creature of ambiguity. A being of righteousness is never comfortable with shades of gray. You would have crossed a line at some point, and he would have inevitably tried to stop you. You would have resented him and his abilities. In your envious state, you would have tried to claim them for your own." The voice of Malefactor grows near; however, he is still nowhere near the Traveler's field of sight.

"Admittedly or not, you are a prideful creature, Traveler. You seek a gateway that will surely lead you to other sinister evils, such as the overindulgence of power. Although pride is considered the most dangerous of all sins, it is not your biggest flaw.

"Notwithstanding your many faults, I was more than willing to establish an alliance. After all, we do share common enemies. However, there is something I cannot overlook. Even after all your martyrdom, you are still a creature guided by faith, and faith is the most dishonest position a creature capable of reason can adopt.

"For me, a being who surrenders the truth to make sense through quaint dogmatic teachings, a believer in the spiritual muffling of facts beyond their intellectual comprehension, is someone who can be fooled into doing almost anything. That makes you untrustworthy. After knowing the truth, you cannot be honest and have faith at the same time," says Malefactor as he pulls back the head of the paralyzed Traveler and kisses his forehead.

"From this point forward, we are what is in our nature to be. Enemies. Fair well, Traveler. We'll see each other soon." The Traveler's sight fades to pure darkness, and the words of Malefactor are but an echo in the distance.

Book of Vouchsafed: Prelude

"Are you not going to say anything?"

"Where am I? I cannot see whatsoever."

"The same place you started your quest for answers—a hole in the Universe. A bottomless void deprived of stars and filled with darkness. Don't you remember?"

"Here in this place, I was taken. I have since suffered many woes, and the truth still eludes me."

"You had but a taste of the suffering that is the sin of existing, born with an inherited predisposition of being hated. Those like me, condemned to an eternity in oblivion for sins of the same kind, have nothing more to do than observe and reflect. You might find that the most villainous of all creatures are often the most sincere."

"Yes, I just met someone who professed the same."

"You have to finally open yourself up to the possibilities that not everything is what it should be. Can you do that?"

"I can. I have questions that still need answers."

"And I have the answers to the questions you haven't even thought of yet. Ask away, Traveler."

"I want you to finish your tale. Who are you?"

An excerpt from The Book of Bedlam

THE GODSLAYER

THE NATURAL ORDER OF THINGS severed the Known Universe's direct opposite, the destructive force known as The Unhallowed, into two. The split created what is now known as the Void. It also gave birth to something of supreme power. Reduced to a frail framework of a hominid nature, Death could not help but stare at her palms, cracking her long, bony fingers as she flexed and extended them in a disturbing, ritualistic manner. She felt raped, hollowed out by the sheer might of usurpers. As a token of mercy, her newfound naked existence was wrapped in an elegantly long, flowing, hooded robe, which decayed into ragged clothing of faded dark at the touch of her skin. There was no getting used to her newfound reality. Nonsensical whispers echoed all around her as if each of her thoughts had a voice of its own.

"What have I become? They did this! Left me this way!"

"Smell that?"

"Yes, false-god blood. It smells sweet."

"Bring back the darkness! Kill them all!"

Her incoherent mumblings caught the attention of the embodiment of Vengeance of the Natural Order of Things.

When she approached Death to urge her into her new role within the Known Universe, Death turned her hooded head slowly toward the root of her misfortune. Within her pale white eyes, a pair of dark blotches acted as her irises. The swirling vortexes were devoid of consciousness's fundamental elements, scruples, or a moral sense. There was no rudimentary understanding to be found. These black abysses were filled only with deep, dark rage and malice. As she flashed an ominous grin, she produced something most sinister.

Forged from the fossil of a primordial beast, the massive curved sickle was a wonder to behold. The glowing cryptic writings carved across the blade adorned the terrifying mortal instrument by emitting a malevolent spark. These were the first chronicled words in existence, and since they were chiseled into being, no one has dared utter them aloud. Welded to the opposite side of the blade, the skull of a nightmarish creature acted as a heel. The skull's jaw was unhinged as if the beast cried one final primal scream, a shriek muffled by what can only be imagined was the result of grim death. Connected to the skull base, the creature's warped spine acted as a snath for the blade, and a femur bone twisted violently into the backbone served as a grip.

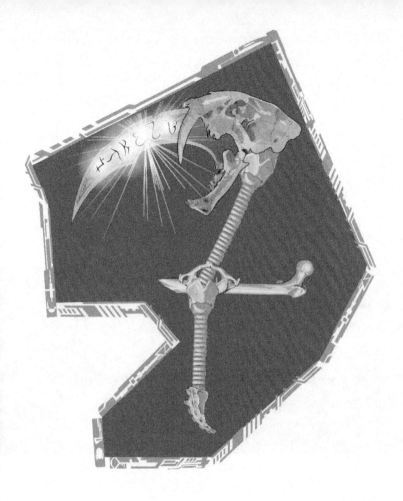

As the aspect of Wrath came closer, Death spoke to her with utmost irreverence.

"I am a slave to no god!"

Death scythed the blade westward in the most combative manner, ripping into the abdomen of the embodiment of Vengeance of the Natural Order of Things with ease. A discharge of cosmic

energy detonated across the cosmos, followed by a baleful chuckle from the assailant and a collective cry from the remaining threesome. This was how the foursome deity became a trinity. As she hemorrhaged her last iota of energy, Vengeance's being was reduced to a clinging mummified corpse. Like a parasitic twin, she adhered to the trinity's back as a useless crippled carcass. This was one of the many ominous changes the Natural Order of Things went through.

He stares at the darkness and listens attentively. Etching each word I speak into his consciousness. This is not the same petulant creature I first encountered. The Traveler has changed.

As was expected, the aspect of Compassion became grief-stricken as her head hung in sorrow, and tears of starlight were born in her lustrous eyes. They rolled down her enamel cheeks and withered away with a glorious burst on her lips. It was at that moment that her inner glow wavered. However, true to her role, she understood that this new concoction's bestial nature reacted accordantly with her character. For it is in her

heart to have an endless desire to ease others' suffering, her sympathetic consciousness replaced any ill will toward Death.

Although saddened by Vengeance's death, Absolution's reaction was entirely dissimilar to that of the facet of Compassion. His resolve was more commanding than ever. His role within the Natural Order of Things became more systematic in reasoning and less influenced by living things' empathy. As the acquittal device held in his hand came down, it became clear that no measure of absolution would be awarded for Death on his behalf.

The most significant perceptible changes occurred to the most prominent of all remaining aspects of this first deity. The embodiment of Judgment became vindictive. Beleaguered with an overwhelming flow of painful memories of Vengeance's demise, he became infected with something most sinister. Judgment's form absorbed most of Vengeance's unpleasant traits, such as her temperament and thirst for reprisal. He unleashed at Death with great vengeance. The collective force of the Natural Order of Things' remaining constituents managed to subdue Death's fury.

The embodiment of Death was halted; however, her impact on life's equation could not be undone. It was so that the manifestation of Judgment spoke directly to her.

"I say to you, death-bringer, you shall be bound and shackled forevermore until a day comes when you learn to abide by our laws."

An interstellar prison was created, revealed to you by the creature known as Daystar. The jail proved to be foolproof and inescapable.

"With this sigil, I bind thee. You shall be compelled to see and grasp the miracle of life and the suffering you've unleashed upon this Universe. There, you shall remain for eons until the day comes when we release you to take life away once more, and you will be compelled to do so with great sorrow."

Death was jailed like a rabid beast. Trapped within an inflationary zone within the Known Universe, she will stew in her anger, tormented by solitude until the end of time. An ancient lock, concocted of a powerful curse infused on a cryptic, circular seal, that emblem in your pocket, will be the only device that will stand between her and her freedom.

"Why do you refer to yourself in the third person? It is clear to me who you are."

"Because that was long ago. I am but a shadow of what I once was, Traveler. All the players in this plane of existence are but ever-evolving creatures. Only fools let who they once were, prevent who they are now from turning into what they want to become. I am not the bestial instrument of destruction I once was, nor you the same naïve, dogmatic fool."

"In the Kingdom, I saw three massive sculptures. They seemed to be tributes to great figures of utmost importance. All were defaced and vandalized. It would seem that the space reserved for a fourth one was sealed off, erased from history. I had the misfortune of meeting one of them. Thus far, all clues within the Kingdom prove your story true. If one dies by your hand, what happens to the other two?"

Faced with their own mortality, a morbid, persistent feeling of dread and apprehension overcame the Natural Order of Things. They felt an emotion that, until now, was ascribed only to mortal beings. They felt fear.

With the utmost prominent embodiment of chaos trapped forever in a cage, the Known Universe's balance was once again askew. The Natural Order of Things sought to establish order once more. This time, however, their involvement will not be firsthand. Thanatophobia rules over them. They solve their dilemma by creating nonfigurative entities that police the two principal aspects of balance within The Known Universe, Chaos and Order.

The Universal Bylaw, known as the Fates, proved to be a destructive phenomenon. From their conception, they had spread a disease that had been nearly impossible to contain and unachievable to eradicate.

"Yes, I've been found guilty of the transgressions of my people."

"No Traveler, your sin might be by birthright, but it's not entirely your fault."

"And by that, you mean what exactly?"

"As everything in the natural order has its purpose, The Natural Order of Things was born as an intermediary force to balance the Known Universe. They became corrupted after our encounter, as fear became a gateway for other mortals' unpleasant behaviors. The despotic rule of the aspect of Judgment sealed off their utmost opposition. They wanted to maintain a semblance of control, and they broke a fundamental rule in their misguidance. They subdue the Known Universe to poise themselves as the supreme power and sublet their primary task by creating minions to carry out their behest. In their hubris, they forgot that only the Known Universe is capable of creating life. With the birth of your species, the first paradox came into being."

"It was him! My creator is the cause of all this."

"Yes. However, your species made it worse in the long run by following in your father's footsteps and creating living creatures of your own. The aspect of Judgment, known to few as Helō'hēm and Lord of Host to others, is the architect behind the Nocuous Plague. He created the first carcinogenic paradox by breathing life into your kind, a sin he pinned on your species as he ascended himself to the role of omniscient, silencing the voice of The Known Universe."

"What role did the other two have in this coup?"

"Very little, I'm afraid. The aspects of Compassion and Absolution helped with the architecture of your species' role. However, their involvement subsequently proved to be minimal. The element of Judgment became totalitarian.

"As Helō'hēm ascended into power, Nēt'zach, the facet of Compassion, became increasingly dejected. Her bond with all living things attuned her to the lament and wail of The Known Universe. While the toxic paradoxes caused the Universe insufferable pain, its cries made her fall into a profound abyss of melancholy. The totalitarian rule of Helō'hēm caused her to detach from the trinity. She traveled far away from one corner of The Universe to the next to find solace. It has been said that, in time, The Universe gathered with her. She devised a viable solution. However, before she could enact her intentions, she was found out.

"Uri'Gō, the face of Absolution, was sent by Helō'hēm to pass judgment onto her for her disconnect and abandonment. Uri'Gō stood before her with his acquittal device in hand, ready to give a sentence. It was so that the most beautiful creature in creation pleaded her case to her brother."

"What became of her?"

"To make amends for her sins, Nēt'zach, the facet of Compassion, relinquished her own life to create a place to absorb and contain most of the carcinogenic paradoxes onto herself. She became Gaɪə, the third planet from a distant solar system isolated from other sectors."

"She felt it was her fault and took the pain onto herself. What happened to her brother?"

"Uri'Gō returned to Helō'hēm with the news of what had transpired. The newly crowned god became enraged and asked why he did not stop her. To which Uri'Gō replied that she had sidestepped their will as she passed judgment onto herself. For the most part, the aspect of absolution had always lacked any emotional expression. This time, he smiled and confessed to his brother that he would have done the same in her place.

"Indeed, this is an event to mourn, for, on this day, I pass judgment onto one of my own. My brother, advocate for all Universal life, I find thee guilty of the treasonous act of conspiring against the welfare of the Universe. Guilty of circumventing the will of the Natural Order of Things by abetting a traitor to abandon her birthright duties, infringing upon the will of the Natural Law.

"I hereby strip you of your boon and glory and sentence you to commune among the living. On the third planet of an inconsequential system, where our grieving sister forfeited her life, you will serve as the embodiment of sacrifice. You will be reborn time and again with no memory of who you were but with a clear mission. To face pain, suffering, and death, the wicked may find redemption, and among the mundane, luminaries will rise by your teachings to improve their race. On the day you forsake your destiny, halting the rise of Luminaries, you will know that I will unleash my final judgment upon all, including you and what has become of your sister."

"Similar to the fate of the Unhallowed, Helō'hēm stripped Uri'Gō of most of his abilities and condemned him to die and be reborn in perpetuity for the sins of the mortals chosen to live on the newfound planet that once was Nēt'zach, the facet of Compassion."

"What are luminaries?"

"Flawed mortal creatures of inherent goodness that follow a doctrine composed of moral values that serve as an example for the betterment of the populace around them. Martyrs worthy of praise who are destined to delay the course of the unavoidable derailment of their species."

"So, it is all for nothing?"

"Not quite, Traveler. The facet of Compassion, who became Gaɪə, communicated with the otherwise muffled Universe. With the help of her brother Uri'Gō, they concocted a plan that would go unforeseen even to the now omniscient Helō'hēm. They knew that Helō'hēm had an obsessive admiration for those born out of natural order, something the Known Universe can create that he has not the power to replicate.

"When she morphed into Gaɪə, she called upon Uri'Gō to collect artifacts belonging to the utmost creations of The Fates, the false gods. Meanwhile, The Universe seeded her with humanoids to populate it. A world that served as a balance between those who meant to be with strategically placed unearthly artifacts.

"In her world, as creatures of enlightenment, of natural birth, and fueled by anima come forth, they are given the innate ability to affect reality by the way they process strange phenomena. A singular person can alter the conjectured state of things as they exist. When introduced with an alternate reality, rather than the collective consensus of how it may seem or might be imagined, there are two possible causal effects.

"As you know, a direct and disturbing manifestation of paranormal proportions results in the birth of paradoxes. At the same time, the advent of a subtle welcoming event that the susceptible-minded find inexplicable by natural law is considered the work of divine intervention, but is known as *Axiom Particles*."

"Axiom Particles? Never heard of them."

"Of course you have, Traveler. However, you know them as miracles—the answer to a mortal's plea for intervention directed to a higher power. Naturally, these miracles are the unrecognized result of mankind's own doings or unexpected actions.

"Nevertheless, the strategically placed artifacts served a purpose. They strayed the natural evolutionary process of the third planet's habitats from a logistic preponderance of what's real, proven by a reasoning system over the false beliefs of feeble-minded beings that often lack rationality.

"They became creatures of faith that hold on to credence without the necessity of an evidentiary warrant. Through lazy pondering, the mud-monkeys, known as humankind, sought a way to give sense to their now meaningless lives. They gave the artifacts a backstory that grew exaggerated as it was passed on to future generations. When the burden of their existence proved to be too much to bear, they sought aid through prayers. They call on higher beings to assist them with their mundane existence. The artifacts fuel their imagination of celestial forces that cater to their plights.

"When their prayers went unanswered, and their problems multiplied, it became simpler to rest the blame on an enemy they could fight instead of a plethora of bad decisions and inactions on their part. With no actual otherworldly interventions, there are no paradoxes to be made. Whatever the case, the adjoined union between what "should be" and what "should not" had the sought-out effect of the Axiom Particles."

"What is the intended effect of the Axiom Particle?"

"Simple. The Axiom Particles seek out and attach themselves to paradoxes, penetrate their membranes, and destabilize their core, rendering them inert."

"Humans had been given tremendous power then. The difference between breaking reality and bending it implies inflicting an illness or curing it—all resulting from thought and interpretation. I don't know if I should feel at ease or scared, Ghost."

"You will soon find out with your new given role, Traveler. The status quo has changed, and not for the better. The release of your enemy will guarantee the return of many things that should have remained buried and forgotten. The third planet's intended purpose of a healing cell will become obsolete as it will become the center of an upcoming war that will wager for the survival of everything that now exists. You, Traveler, will find yourself amidst everything."

"How can you be sure that I will follow the path laid out before me, Ghost?"

"Because I know the outcome of all that is, was, and will be, Traveler."

"Are you going to tell me that you, a prisoner of the heavens, read the covenant book that was once safeguarded by the most powerful creatures in the universe? A book whose content twisted the mind of one of the purest creatures in the Universe into Malefactor, a being of unadulterated evil? You read that book from your tiny cell?"

"The item you refer to is a singular artifact that physically manifests concurrently at a multiversal level. All alterations to its content are reflected simultaneously at a multidimensional level regardless of whichever plane of existence it takes place. To answer your question, not only have I read it, Traveler, I am its author. That's how I know that the days ahead of you would turn those you lived in torment and agony into nostalgic memories of better days."

"I have already decided what my path will be, Ghost. What remains unclear to me is your role in all of this."

"The same as you, Traveler. I'm but a pawn in a very complicated plot."

"You could have chosen anyone in the Universe to divulge all of this too. Why choose me?

"Because as I said, in the grand scheme of life, we all have a part to play, and you are destined to deliver my freedom, Traveler."

"You must think of me as someone that's gone mad! Why would I entertain the notion of unleashing the very thing that will be more dangerous than any of the threats the Universe is currently facing? Do you genuinely believe a bonding experience over a tale of an uncertain truth will sway me to take pity on you and set you free, Ghost?"

"Certainly not. It is not me who pleads for freedom. There will come a time of great desperation, a pivotal moment where all will seem lost. On that day, you will beg for my help, and against my better judgment, I will agree to roam the Universe once more."

"I will never agree to that, Ghost. Your tale has proven to be true until now, as I see it for what it is, a ploy for your freedom. You may deny it, but like all the others I have encountered, you are a liar."

"Except for Malefactor, all the creatures you have encountered offer and defend the boon of life, a gift disguised as a curse filled with plights and suffering. I offer only death—a release from the shell that keeps creatures imprisoned from their true forms. One is a lie disguised as beautiful truth, as mine is an undeniable yet frightening reality. Go now, Traveler. Earth awaits."

"Fair well, Death. I doubt we'll see each other again."

A single Traveler breezes through the vastness of space, fiercely determined. He finally possesses the sought-out answers that had eluded him all this time. He leaves behind what he was and reluctantly embraces what he has become. The gravelly voice that once haunted him is now but an earworm that reverberates within his head. His mission is to maintain balance within all aspects of life, guide humanity into a new age of prosperity, and eradicate the paradoxes that threaten the Known Universe. His days of having the power to control gods and mortals' fortunes are gone, and his newfound abilities pale in comparison. This will seem like an insurmountable task for him to carry out, especially for someone sidetracked by the amount of vengeance that resides within him. If he only knew what Malefactor has done in his absence. If he realized what lay ahead, his newfound heart would sink. His enemy has ripped a gash in the fabric of reality. The old gods have returned to reclaim what is rightfully theirs, and all sorts of nightmarish creatures roam about. If I had a soul, I would pity him."

Made in the USA
Columbia, SC
06 July 2023

19608883R00104